FOSSICKER'S GULLY

When journalist Amy Randall is abducted at gunpoint by her sister-in-law, Kelly, and left in an old mine tunnel to die, she is lucky to escape. Allowing Kelly to believe her sinister plan has succeeded, Amy goes into hiding to investigate. Local policeman Alex Hammond, her childhood crush and her brother's lifelong friend, agrees to help, and offers Amy a place to stay at his flat. What is Kelly hiding, and why does she seem bent on revenge against the Randall family? It's a race to uncover the truth before Kelly finds a new victim, and meanwhile, Amy and Alex draw closer. Set in a small town in the central Victorian goldfields, *Fossicker's Gully* throws old friends together, brings new love, and reveals a heartwarming family secret.

NOELENE JENKINSON

FOSSICKER'S GULLY

Complete and Unabridged

AURORA
Leicester

First published in Great Britain in 2020

First Aurora Edition
published 2020

The moral right of the author has been asserted

A catalogue record for this book is available
from the British Library.

ISBN 978–1–78782–472–0

Published by
Ulverscroft Limited
Anstey, Leicestershire

Set by Words & Graphics Ltd.
Anstey, Leicestershire
Printed and bound in Great Britain by
T. J. International Ltd., Padstow, Cornwall

This book is printed on acid-free paper

1

Amy Randall sped in her silver compact SUV away from the main street of Fossicker's Gully, one of many small country townships founded upon the discovery of gold in central Victoria.

Chinese had puddled here, Californians had sailed across the Pacific from their own gold strike fields, and Europeans of every nationality all came hoping to make a fortune.

She turned onto the boundary road at the edge of her hometown, fondly known by locals as the Gully, and the familiar gravelled track that led to her cabin. Edged by the region's box ironbark eucalypts that characterised the many nature reserves in the district, she loved the peppermint-scented bush and had bought her little home sanctuary for its privacy and seclusion amid nature.

Amy savoured her regular runs along the forest trails through the understorey of wattles, small shrubs and grasses, each pocket of bushland known by the locals with such names as Deadman's Gully and Nowhere Creek, relics of bygone mining days.

Where once the air had rung with the sounds of pioneers and gold diggers, it now echoed only with the calls of birds and animals, the woodland ecosystem producing nectar and pollen all year. It was an especially important feeding habitat for the green swift parrots with their red faces and purple tails that bred in the Tasmanian summer before migrating across Bass Street to the mainland in autumn. Over winter they nested in tree hollows and feasted on the nectar of the large flowering ironbark blossoms.

A local survey had identified the species as critically endangered, but one would never guess as they noisily screeched, swooping and weaving through the treetops.

Today, Amy was keen to get home. Not only because it was Friday and a weekend stretched gloriously ahead, although as always she had nothing specifically planned, but because the weather forecast predicted a cold change with rain so she needed to shut the windows she left open before leaving for work this morning in the newspaper office of the *Gully Standard*.

Besides, she had agreed to an unexpected meeting and needed to be early to emotionally prepare. Amy and her sister-in-law, Kelly, simply did not click. Nursing a healthy dose of instinctive mistrust for the woman until someone proved otherwise, she knew they never would.

She relaxed as she glimpsed her weathered timber cabin sitting casually square and low, nestled perfectly into its surroundings. It had taken over a year, but the rusting roofing iron had been replaced and indoors was now lovingly scrubbed, painted and restored into cosy bachelor-girl digs appropriate for the climate and her busy single lifestyle.

And Kelly's vehicle was nowhere in sight. Good. She had time to breathe.

But as Amy drove around the cabin to park in

her garage at the back, her mood deflated. Kelly's sporty pink car, always totally recognisable around town, was already here. Odd. The rare times she visited, she usually parked out front.

Amy sighed. Stephen sure indulged his petite trophy wife. Maybe it was because they didn't have any children. Her brother hid his disappointment but before marriage had always talked of sons to inherit and continue the family transport business.

Although Amy believed her sister-in-law came with baggage, she hadn't come with a fortune. She had married money instead. Compliments of their Randall ancestors, early carters to the goldfields, the transport company now transformed into a trucking empire, capably co-managed by her lawyer brother, Stephen, but fiercely controlled by their dominant father, David.

Amy drew in a deep breath for strength as she stepped from her car, dragged her shoulder bag and laptop case off the rear seat, and strode for the house. She climbed the back steps and with a forced smile walked inside to bear up against this surprise unwelcome visit. It occurred to her that she really should start locking up the cabin. Maybe she would do that from now on.

'Hi,' she greeted her sister-in-law as she dumped her belongings on the kitchen bench.

Kelly's bleached blonde hair, makeup, jewellery and matching clothes were all in place. As usual. But she didn't normally wear gloves. Weird, although the weather had already turned unseasonably colder and would no doubt grow worse after the icy blast from a forecast weekend front swept across the state in this notoriously chilly inland region. Which only meant the milder seasons were all the more warmly greeted when they arrived.

'You're early.' Amy tried to sound pleased.

'Yes. Thought I would surprise you.'

Amy frowned. 'Not really. I *was* expecting you.' Something was even more *off* than usual in her attitude.

'Okay,' Amy said slowly. 'Give me a moment, I need to close some windows.'

The ground floor was protected by its fully surrounding veranda, so Amy only needed to dash upstairs, close the sashes and return below. Because her mind was distracted and churning over the possible reason for the impending conversation, Amy halted in shock as she descended and reached the bottom step a few minutes later.

To face her visitor pointing the barrel of a handgun directly at her.

Amy recognised the gun. It belonged to her brother. A sporting shooter who took part in monthly competitive target shooting, the only way a private person could legally own such a firearm.

Her heart skipped a beat in dread and sank with fear at the same time. 'What the hell is this?'

'Revenge.' Kelly's ice-blue eyes glared with excitement, both gloved hands on the gun alarmingly steady.

Amy considered the situation beyond scary. It was lethal. And yet she had always forced herself to be abnormally polite to the woman, if only because she was her adored brother's wife.

'Why? What have I ever done to you?'

'You are so ignorant,' she scoffed, shaking her head. 'Your stupid family has been so blind and trusting.'

So this was about the Randalls, then. Clearly serious stuff and well planned.

'To what?' Amy swallowed down her dry throat, not daring to move, clenching her fists at her sides.

'You'll never know because you're first.' She waved the point of the gun toward the door. 'Get your keys and go out to the car.'

Did she intend shooting her out in the bush? And then would she go after someone else in the family? Who? Stephen? Her parents?

'Move! Before it rains.'

Amy's mind buzzed. Right. To hide tracks. This woman was driven and smart. All nicely hidden beneath that helpless female exterior that had fooled the whole Randall family for years. Ignorant of the reason behind this sinister intent, no way would she be an easy target. She was fit and would pick her moment.

Annoyed at Amy's hesitation, Kelly snapped, 'Now!'

Amy walked to the kitchen bench, the hairs all over her body standing on end, aware a gun was pointed at her back. She fished out the car keys from her shoulder bag and headed for the door.

'Slowly!'

Treading carefully as instructed, Amy moved outside toward her vehicle and slid behind the wheel while Kelly sat in the back seat.

'Drive to the tunnel.'

Shit. Was she going to be murdered in the old mine drive? Well at least she knew she would be alive until then. It didn't take long. The tunnel was nearby in the heart of the nature reserve.

'Out!' Kelly demanded as they pulled up.

From her voice and skyward glances, Amy sensed her captor was growing antsy. She was really relying on that rain. Amy hoped it didn't come. She might be killed, but at least there would be tracks. Evidence.

With the gun still pointed at Amy, Kelly halted before the grated tunnel gate. 'Open it.'

'It's locked.'

'No it's not.'

Peering closer, Amy noticed the lock hook had already been released, still marvelling amidst her growing terror that pretentious, chic Kelly was hard and cool enough to plan all this. Her mind whirled only for a moment over how she had obtained a key to unlock the tunnel gate. Then she remembered Kelly had joined the local historical society and helped lead occasional mining tunnel tours here, so she would have legitimate access to this off-limits and padlocked abandoned site.

All for this purpose? Brilliant strategy, if it wasn't so alarming in its premeditated purpose. Stalling, Amy pushed the gate barely ajar.

'Wider!'

Amy heaved, the hinges stiff and rusty with age. When it was half open, Kelly stepped closer and shoved her from behind, and she stumbled through. Ahead lay only darkness.

'Walk!'

'I can't see a thing.' Amy paused, hedging for time.

'Move!'

Amy gingerly trod one careful step at a time, one foot in front of the other, focusing so heavily on not falling over or breaking an ankle on fallen rocks or holes in the ground that she didn't realise Kelly hadn't followed until she heard her voice from a distance behind.

'Stop!'

Amy wondered if she dared run. If she couldn't see Kelly, Kelly couldn't see her. But she would need to turn around to distinguish that. So she did.

'Stay there!'

Kelly's dark silhouette was outlined against the tunnel entrance further behind, and her arm was raised to fire the gun. Amy began to tremble. Was this it?

The gun fired, the noise of its resounding blast bouncing back off the walls. Amy instinctively ducked but felt nothing. Kelly had missed! But before she could react and move, another shot rang out, and this time it hits its mark.

Amy screeched and clutched her shoulder as she was gripped with biting pain while the second boom echoed back through the underground space. Disoriented and with her ears ringing, she saw Kelly turn and run but heard no sound of her footfalls on the ground. Amid the stinging pain and strange echoed sensations in her head, she suddenly realised she was deaf.

7

Dazed, Amy stumbled against a wall, wincing at her searing shoulder, confused in her now silent world. All of her resistance collapsed, she felt sick, and her world faded.

Much later, as Amy slowly emerged from her dark unconscious place, it took a moment for her senses to gather. Then she remembered she was in the old abandoned gold mining tunnel, forced here at gunpoint by Kelly, with its iron gate presumably securely locked again and no way out.

The agony in her left shoulder took her breath away. At such close range, Amy was astounded that even a city person like Kelly would miss a sure shot. Which only got her thinking maybe it was intentional. To make her suffer?

Had Kelly left her here to die, perhaps believing if the gunshot didn't do the trick, exposure to the elements surely would? She had underestimated Amy's physical fitness and resilience. For a time, she rested, gathering strength, pressing hard on her wound. No point looking to investigate the extent of the damage. She could barely see a thing.

Later, Amy tried to heave herself to her feet but grew lightheaded and faint, forcing her to sink to the hard, cold tunnel floor before the world went dark again.

As she once more slowly became conscious — how much later, she had no idea — and shivered with cold, she heard trickling water. From a thin shaft of light somewhere much higher above filtering down, she saw small glistening rivulets curving their way over the tunnel sides to the floor. Runoff from the forecast rain against which she had shut the cabin windows.

Keeping to dry ground, Amy shuffled closer to the mini-stream. In agony, she strained her injured shoulder as she reached out, leaning forward to awkwardly cup and slurp up small handfuls of cold, refreshing rainwater.

When she mustered the strength to stand, balancing against the wall and pushing through her pain, Amy slowly hobbled toward the locked tunnel entrance gate, the only other faint light. Even as she began to cry out, she knew it was useless. In an isolated bush reserve only used by a few locals, tourist bush walkers or gold panners in the creek even on a sunny day, certainly no sensible human would venture out in this foul weather.

But Amy, ever the optimist, kept calling out at intervals anyway between bouts of nausea and drifts of dizziness.

Barely aware and shaking, whether from shock or the tunnel's icy cold, she knew she desperately needed to get warm. A pipe dream like the heady thought of a good, long sleep.

She considered using one of the many small rocks to try and bash at the tunnel entrance gate lock but simply couldn't gather the energy. She felt bruised and weak all over from the fall when she'd fainted after the gunshot.

In her state of semiconsciousness and brain fog, Amy's thoughts turned to who might realise she was missing. Her social life was non-existent and she had made no plans. Apart from leaving work and her fateful arranged meeting with Kelly, no one would be looking for her until she didn't show up for work on Monday.

Monday. She might survive till then, despite the cold and damp, but she worried over her injury that surely needed attention.

The heavy rain clouds covered any possible moonlight, and Amy presumed it was long since dark anyway. So, apart from faint half-light at the tunnel entrance, she finally gave up on calling for help. No one would be about.

Feeling her way along the walls, groaning with pain and the weakening sickness of shock, she settled further back in the tunnel and just around a small bend away from the wind gusting in through the grilled gate opening. Huddling herself into a ball and uncovered against the bitter night, attempting but failing to keep warm, Amy tried to sleep.

Moments of shooting pain dragged soft moans from her, keeping her mostly conscious, but she only managed to doze in short bursts, waking with sharp bouts of coughing. Whether from her injury, the biting cold or the hard ground beneath, Amy neither knew nor cared. The long uncomfortable night stretched out like a bad dream and became a nightmare.

★ ★ ★

Kelly Randall smirked to herself as she drove Amy's car back to the cabin, parked it in the garage and drove her own car home. Too easy.

Her bitch sister-in-law was never getting out of

10

that hole alive. If she didn't bleed to death from the gunshot wound, she certainly would from exposure in the icy unprotected passageway over the weekend.

As lightning flashed across the threatening sky and thunder rumbled overhead, Kelly mentally rubbed her hands together, speeding back through the darkening dusk to the luxurious townhouse she shared with her loving, insipid husband.

Such good fortune that the weakling man was an enthusiastic sporting shooter. His pastime had sown the first seeds of her plan. Kelly appreciated he went through a lot to secure his licence. To her benefit. Lots of safety training and probation with his local club, police approval and registration. If she remembered rightly, the whole process took almost a year. Handy that he chose a revolver instead of a pistol. It had been so dim in the tunnel that as soon as she squeezed the trigger, she knew her aim had been slightly off and she would need a second shot.

Her first priority back at home was to return the four remaining bullets into the cartridge box, wipe the weapon clean and lock it up again in Stephen's gun safe.

Steadying her poise with deep breaths and a glass of her favourite ruby claret, Kelly Randall preened as she put the final touches to dinner and awaited her husband's return. She had achieved a successful afternoon's work and thrilled with a tinge of excitement to know her long-held plan was underway at last.

Recent years had felt like forever as they trickled by and tested her patience while she quietly fostered pity and traded on sympathy for her past, biding her time.

Oh yes, in marrying Stephen Randall, the son and heir, she had not misjudged her prey. Once chosen, he had proved the perfect means to achieve her purpose.

Having disposed of her first hurdle this afternoon, now spicy wafts of her husband's favourite curry drifted around the designer kitchen of the townhouse she had successfully begged him to build to her specifications. The title of which she had convinced him, for tax reasons of course, would be wise to place into her name alone. The fool man had even praised her for the suggestion.

Although Fossicker's Gully was a godforsaken backwater, the Randall townhouse property was immaculately furnished and presented. Making it easy for her to obtain a mortgage for almost its full value, no questions asked. And about which Stephen knew nothing.

Flowers graced the antique dining table and chubby lit candles flickered for the intimate ambience she always deliberately chose to create. Stephen might work in a busy office organising those dirty great trucks all day, but at heart he was a romantic, so at every opportunity she fed his ego. Keeping him sexually happy was a distasteful duty she endured for the greater good of her ultimate goal — payback, independence and freedom.

She sighed, admiring her handiwork. All was

perfect. As she liked it.

Kelly knew her own inherent weaknesses. She didn't like falling short in any way or being unfairly judged. From the moment they married and moved into this magnificent house, Stephen had offered to hire a housekeeper, but Kelly objected. Being a perfectionist, she needed everything around her sparkling clean and tidy. Just so. No noisy children. No messy pets. Just her and Stephen, who was not only her path to comfort but the vehicle for revenge.

Since learning the truth of her father's desertion and feeling unwanted as a child, she always strove to do better. Burdened with inadequacy because of her poor background and attempting to compensate by trying to please people. But with her husband, of course, it was for a reason.

No one would be looking for her dead or dying sister-in-law, locked away and rotting in the tunnel, at least until Monday. Plus she had the bonus of the predicted steady downpour of late autumn rain now deliciously washing away all evidence of footprints and car tracks.

It would take time for gullible sentimental Stephen to grieve for his sister, but when the time was right, he was next. Timing and place would be vital. Getting him interested in her, falling in love and the security of a wedding ring on her finger had been too easy. Achieved without a hitch due to her dedication to the scheme and meticulous mind for detail.

Stephen's demise would entitle her to at least one third of a thriving transport empire. She had searched in his briefcase, brought home with nightly diligence from the company office so her conscientious husband could work late. The papers and accounts all revealing enormous sums of money. Capital worth. Investments.

Millions.

She had almost fainted in shock. Even now her heart palpitated at the memory of those first discoveries her eyes had seen, leaving her gasping.

Of course divorce was always a tempting option, but by removing the two young heirs of the next generation, her reward would be far greater and much more satisfactory. She knew it was greedy, but it was not only her own financial future at stake. Someone else was involved, so dear to her heart, who deserved nothing less than absolute justice.

There was no rush. She had waited over ten years, biding her time for a purpose, waiting for this opportunity ever since as a teenager her probing questions had finally yielded the truth from her mother. Kelly had promptly set a scheme in motion, moved to Fossicker's Gully and after a bizarre and heady courtship which both excited and repulsed her, three years ago landed the jackpot marriage she desired.

Her true identity and explanation of her past had never been doubted or challenged, so she was safe.

The Randalls thought wealth and social standing elevated them above everyone else, making them untouchable. Kelly smirked to herself. They were about to learn otherwise and

14

suffer, while she walked away the winner with her rightful share of the spoils, reaping long overdue rewards.

When her pathetic husband Stephen arrived home thirty minutes later, she suffered his habitual loving kiss.

Tonight, however, as he removed his coat and hung it neatly on the entry hallway stand as she expected, he frowned in concern. 'Is everything okay, my sweet?'

From habit and caution, Kelly always thought before responding, making sure to carefully choose her words. More than once, her restraint had smoothed a situation.

'Of course, my love. Why do you ask?'

'You seem distracted.' Were her excitement and adrenalin showing? 'I hope it's nothing I've said or done,' he added.

Kelly appreciated the way he tended to place blame upon himself for almost any disharmony between them. By staying amenable, those times were rare.

'Oh my love, of course not. It would never be you.'

She injected just the right amount of conviction into her lowered silky voice, slid her arms about his waist and snuggled against him in reassurance, relaxing, knowing all was on the path to being well.

'And I'm fine. Thank you so much for asking.'

Oh, how much longer could she keep up this sickening pretence?

'You're such a good man to care for me and are always concerned for my welfare.' She managed a small theatrical sigh. 'But perhaps I am a little tired lately. I have a lot on my mind, as you know, what with being the chairperson again on the annual charity fundraiser with your mother.' The upcoming event had been a perfect cover of late. 'And my community volunteer work, too.' She drew away from him and said earnestly, 'But I'm more than happy to give my time, because I know it's important to your family to support the town.'

'You're so unselfish, my sweet. Don't forget to look after yourself, too.'

'Oh, I am. It might not always seem like it, but I am fully in charge of my life and my time.'

'Pleased to hear it. You're such a superb homemaker. But just because we only have each other, you know I've always said you can do whatever pleases you.'

'I know. I will. You can be sure of that. You're so generous to me, Stephen. There's not a single moment that I don't bless the day we met.'

2

Amy woke with a fright to hear rattling and footsteps in the tunnel. Alarm washed across her mind as the barest hint of daylight filtered along the mine. Stiff with terror and barely able to move with pain and cold, she feared Kelly had returned. There was no escape.

Barely daring to breathe, she held her breath as the footsteps halted and a bulky dark shadow loomed over her.

'What on earth you doin' in here, girl?'

A man's gravelly voice. Couldn't be Kelly, then. Amy half breathed again with relief and opened her eyes. In the pale early morning light, it was hard to distinguish the identity of her saviour. Until he raised a kero lantern and spoke again.

'You injured, lass?'

Although people rarely heard the old man's warm gravelly tone, Amy would recognise it anywhere.

'Augie?'

God he was a wonderful ugly sight, wrinkled face hidden behind whiskers, his wiry grey hair covered with his familiar tattered old cap.

'That's right, lass. You're the Randall newspaper girl?'

Amy groggily propped herself up on one elbow, hurting as it dug into the dirt beneath. August Temple was a hermit and pretty much

17

the only old local fossicker living off grid in a bush hut, still eking out a living panning for gold. One of few still lured by the thrill of searching for the precious metal and excitement of a find no matter how small. Always looking so destitute, Amy guessed he rarely found success and wondered why he persisted. Perhaps it gave him a purpose in life.

From time to time she might see him as she pounded her daily run through the bush tracks, his only acknowledgement that he had heard or seen her the slightest dip of his head or hand barely raised in a wave.

'What the hell are you doing out in weather like this?' she gasped.

'Best time after rain when the creeks are running fast. Always a chance of washing up bits of gold,' he grunted.

All the locals well knew the creek that snaked around one side of town flowed well after winter rains but might shrink to a sluggish flow or a mere series of billabongs in summer, if not dry up completely in drought.

'Here.' Augie bent over her now and lent a weathered hand to lever under her arm. 'Can you git up, lass?'

Amy closed her eyes, took a deep breath and with the wiry strength of both his arms, her shoulder shot with fresh pain from the movement, she slowly managed to sit upright and rest against a side wall.

'How did you get into the tunnel with the gate locked?'

'Small pair of bolt cutters.' He patted his coat

18

pocket. Eyeing her blood-stained shoulder and wince of pain, he muttered, 'Somebody git at ya, girl?'

She nodded. 'Tried.' And squinted up at him in the gloom. 'What made you come in here?'

Augie shook his head. 'Heard sounds. Moanin' like.'

Amy tried for a grin. 'Well, bless you, Augie. You've saved my life.'

'Livin' in the bush, a body gits a sense for trouble. Coulda been an injured animal.'

He removed his greatcoat and draped it around her shoulders. She smelt its musty dampness but also basked in the pleasure of its weighty inner warmth.

'Is it still raining?'

Augie shook his head. Private and spare with words, Amy was surprised she had managed any conversation with him at all, which usually amounted to little more than a series of grunts on the old man's behalf.

'Soggy underfoot and leaves are drippin'.' His already withered forehead wrinkled into a deeper frown. 'Who done this to you, lass?' he asked so softly she almost didn't hear.

In the wake of an attempt on their life, anyone else might have willingly blurted out the truth and begged him to alert the police. But neither Amy nor Augie had a phone. Amy because she had left her mobile in the cabin and Augie because he didn't own one.

Besides, she had no proof of the attack. Just her word against Kelly. A massive accusation even considering the wound. She couldn't approach Stephen. Loyal to the core, he wouldn't believe even his own sister against his beloved wife.

No. Instinct told Amy to wait, hold back and try to discover the reason behind Kelly's attack. No way should the woman be alerted to the fact that she had survived. It would ensure Amy's safety and lower Kelly's guard.

'Not sure I want to say.'

'Needs reportin'.'

'Not yet.' She could have asked the dear old man to trudge back into town, but Amy had another idea in mind. 'Can you do me a favour, Augie?' He scowled and wavered. Without his help . . . 'Please.'

'All right. Anythin'.'

'You know the public box on the main road the other side of the reserve?' She paused and he stared right through her. 'Could you phone Sergeant Hammond at the police station, please? Tell him where I am, my situation, and that he should make sure he's not followed. And please don't tell a soul about this. She mustn't know I'm alive and free.'

Amy cringed at her small slip the moment the words left her mouth.

Although Augie's gaze sharpened, he muttered, 'I live in the bush. Ain't seen nothin'.'

The irony being, of course, that Alex Hammond, the very man from whom she had deliberately kept her distance, was now, since his return to the Gully, and in the face of her predicament, pretty much the only person who she could turn to and trust. When he came, and

20

he surely would, Amy wondered how that would play out.

As Augie shambled off, she slid to the ground again, pulled the coat about her and waited. She didn't care about her injury or discomfort. She was alive. And a long cold night spent mostly awake between brief fits of sleep and throbbing pain had provided plenty of time to think. She had no intention of going back home again. She'd get to the bottom of this mystery and play her bloody sister-in-law at her own devious game, creating a few waves of her own.

A crazy plan was forming in her head, but she would need Alex on board to carry it out. And proving to be such a damn good diligent community cop since his return to their hometown meant that task was not going to be easy.

The bad boy from the wrong side of town had split the day he finished high school, disappearing for years to resurface six months ago, instantly proving by his actions that he was a transformed individual and model citizen. Establishing a youth group for lost and wayward kids.

As a result, the Gully had re-assessed and embraced their new reborn hometown policeman. Past mistakes set aside.

Amy had always eyed him from afar and smothered the same feelings of adoration she had nurtured all through high school.

Difficult when he and her brother, Stephen, mates growing up, had recently rekindled their friendship. Apart from a few unavoidable and casual encounters plus a memorable interview as a reporter for the *Gully Standard* when Alex first hit town that proved mind-blowingly hard and forced Amy to dredge up every gram of professionalism and maturity she possessed, she continued to secretly admire him from a distance.

She was no longer a giddy teenager and had never chased a man in her life. If they wanted her, showing interest and respect, depending on her level of attraction, she might respond.

So far, to her crushing disappointment, Alex Hammond had shown no curiosity in his mate Stephen Randall's little sister.

Nothing had changed.

★ ★ ★

After Augie left, although Amy sank into misty dozes, she was still aware of dripping water, the unwelcome chilly breeze blowing through the tunnel and the unpleasant silent semi-darkness that settled around her.

Because time crawled when you waited, what seemed like hours was surely far less, so when she heard noise and movement at the gate and in the tunnel, her heart skipped a beat for joy knowing who it might be. All the same, her body tensed just in case. Maybe Kelly was returning for one final deadly shot. Exactly how she planned to defend herself if it proved to be trouble, she had no idea, because she had little strength to resist or fight back.

When she turned at the human approach,

despite daylight behind him, she instantly knew by the size and shape of the man and that easy muscular rolling gait that it was Alex. She had watched him all her life and especially in her teens, so there wasn't much about his mood and features and gestures she didn't know. Recent months had merely updated her memories.

And she remained impressed.

What daylight existed in the shadowy tunnel spread a highlighting gleam on his dark wavy hair. He was physically stunning, but more than that, he owned a controlled reassurance and trust, evident ten years ago, and the biggest relief for Amy today. And all of that gorgeous specimen of manhood was covered in jeans, a hooded sweater and padded rain jacket.

'Amy?' he ventured softly, frowning, not because he didn't instantly recognise her but that he was clearly surprised at her predicament.

'Thanks for coming.'

'Surprised you asked,' he drawled as he hunkered down close and shrugged off a backpack.

'Really?'

'We've hardly spoken in six months.'

If only he knew why. She scrambled for an excuse. 'I guess we're all busy. Where did you get all that stuff?' she asked when he opened up what turned out to be a huge medical kit.

'From Helen at the Medical Centre.' As Amy opened her mouth to complain, he said quickly, 'Don't worry. I paid cash for it and told her it was for a guy at the station we were holding after a fight last night. Said he had a flesh wound and we didn't have enough supplies. She offered to take a look at him herself.'

'She didn't — ?'

'Nope. Stalled her with my charm and a smile.'

He said it with easy humour and humility but didn't look up as he peeled back Augie's greatcoat and unzipped her windcheater. He sucked in a sharp breath. 'Christ, Amy, looks like someone really tried a number on you.' He cleared his throat. 'You're gonna need to lift up that T-shirt.'

So physically close, his steady breath drifting like a grace across her bare skin, Amy said with false confidence, 'Sure,' hoping he couldn't sense her upheaval and heavy breathing, or put it down to her injury and not her reaction to his warm gentle touch and secret lifelong crush.

Without batting an eyelid at her underwear, he turned and whipped out a camera, snapping photos of her upper arm and shoulder for evidence while Amy just gaped. He didn't yet know she had no intention of reporting her attack.

When she shivered in the chilly air, he set the camera aside and dosed out antiseptic solution to gently wash and clean her wound. Amy closed her eyes and winced. She wondered how many women had been on the receiving end of that deliciously heady magic touch.

'My car wasn't outside?' she asked almost breathlessly, sensitive to his touch, which only marginally eased her soreness.

Alex scowled. 'Nope.'

'Didn't think so.' Amy gasped as he gently dried her lacerated injury.

'You're lucky. It's only a damn decent graze. Looking a bit red and angry. Guess it's been burning. Need painkillers?' Alex paused in concern.

Amy nodded. 'When you're done.'

He grinned. 'You're one tough chick.'

'You mean stubborn.'

When she was young, she had been endlessly teased about her contrary nature. Even back then she wondered if her spirited attitude wasn't an attempt to gain his attention.

'You said it.' With two big gentle hands and fierce concentration, he continued working on her shoulder. 'The bullet hasn't caused more than a deep furrow across your skin, but it's still a nasty wound.'

'Thank you,' she whispered.

She wanted to reach out, put her arms around him and be held. Just for comfort. But she didn't want to frighten him off. She'd asked for his help and he'd come. That was enough.

She didn't have anyone in her life right now who was close enough to give her affection. Certainly not a boyfriend in recent times. Her parents had never been into shows of physical affection, and she tactfully kept her distance from Stephen because of Kelly. With good reason, now Amy had proof of the woman's deceit. How she could break that news to her brother had troubled her all night.

Alex somehow managed to staunch the minor bleed and applied a dressing. 'So, who did this?'

She knew he would ask but not with such quiet intent. He was a trained professional, after all. She also knew she would confide the truth. At the very least, she needed to offload by talking about it, and for someone else to know. Just in case. So she began to explain every detail as she remembered it about Kelly's attempted murder.

'That's why I asked about my car. Kelly would have driven it back to my cabin and taken her own car back home.'

Alex shook his head, cursing and muttering as he finished working on her wound and packed up the medical kit while Amy readjusted her clothes.

'Of all people,' he growled. 'My best mate's wife. Mrs. Perfect-in-every-way. Community charmer.'

Amy filled with relief that he believed her and wry amusement at the truth in his honest words that created the image Kelly intentionally presented to the world.

'She said I was the first,' she whispered in distress. 'Stephen lives with her. He'll be in danger now, too.'

'Damn.'

'Alex, I can't say anything to my brother. You know him. He'll be gutted. He adores Kelly. She's his princess.' Amy slumped and whispered, 'I bet she used Stephen's worship to achieve her purpose. Except I don't know what that is. Yet. One thing I do know for sure. Kelly Randall is definitely not unstable. She knew exactly what she was doing. Had it all planned. She mentioned revenge. Seems to hate our family, yet she married into it and didn't explain why. It all happened so fast and I was so stunned, I didn't think to ask. Not that she would have told me.'

Alex handed Amy two pills and a bottle of water. She swallowed them down. 'Thanks. The slicing pain's reduced to a powerful ache now.'

'Good, but you need to take care until you heal.'

'I don't have time for hand holding. I need to find out the reason behind this attack.'

Alex blew out an exasperated breath. 'Sheesh, Amy, you've been seriously injured. It's a deep laceration that possibly needs stitches and definitely warrants medical attention. You'll need weeks to heal. You shouldn't be going anywhere.'

'I can't go home and I can't be seen around town,' she pointed out. 'Kelly thinks I'm dead or dying, so I need to keep it that way. I've got painkillers. I'll be fine.'

Alex gazed at her softly and shook his head. 'You haven't changed, Miss Independent.'

Amy wasn't sure that was a compliment. 'Nothing wrong with that.'

Alex raised his hands in surrender and chuckled, 'Didn't say there was. Not going there.'

She hesitated. 'So you're on board?'

He locked onto her gaze and in an undertone of warning, said, 'As long as it doesn't affect my job or break the law.'

'Of course. Understood.' Amy waited a beat. 'It's her word against mine,' she defended.

'Understand that, but you do have a deep

bullet graze,' Alex pointed out patiently.

'I can't take the risk. She deliberately planned this so she has no doubt covered her tracks.'

'Maybe not. One thing I want to check out before we leave.' He produced his camera and flashlight.

Before they left the mine tunnel, Alex slowly scoured the ground between where he found Amy and the tunnel entrance, retrieving two bullet shells. With tweezers from the medical kit, he handled them carefully and proudly held them up to her. For a fateful breathtaking moment, their gazes locked.

'Just a bit careless. Maybe Kelly was pumped with adrenalin after she shot you and slipped up. I'll bag these as evidence.' He stowed them in the fingers of safety gloves from the medical kit. He checked his wristwatch. 'I'm on duty soon and need to open up the station. If you reckon you can move, where do you need me to take you?'

'I can't use my car and risk being seen by Kelly around town. Presumably she garaged it back at the cabin, so it must stay there.'

'You're right,' Alex admitted. 'Organised criminals plan and follow a precise ritual. Usually feel no regret. If she thinks she's been discovered, Kelly might return here. If she does, she needs to believe the site is undisturbed. So I agree we need to keep you hidden.'

'Thank you,' Amy crowed and with a shrug added, 'I don't have any commitments this weekend, so I won't be missed.'

'I'm sure that's not the case,' he said softly.

'Well,' Amy stumbled over the personal comment, 'not this weekend anyway. So,' she went on, 'I need to find a vehicle — '

'Hell, with that shoulder, you probably can't even drive.'

Amy drew in a deep breath, ignored his concern and continued, ' — to dig into Kelly's family background. I can't go home and use my laptop. I'll have to access records on a public library computer where I can't be traced, and that means heading to Maryborough.' She frowned. 'I need to jump onto this quick smart, Alex. I have no idea how long this is going to take, so I've been thinking. Can you talk to Stephen? He'll pass it on to my folks, but more importantly to Kelly. Mention I'm out of town on research so Mum doesn't worry and Kelly won't grow suspicious?'

'What about your job?'

'That's my cover. I really was heading off for a few days next week on a feature assignment for a future edition. Just tell Stephen you saw me yesterday before I went home from work,' she announced carefully. 'We stopped to chat and I mentioned I was taking off early for a few days. Just be cool. Drop it casually into a conversation. If I need more time in the coming days, I'll phone into the office that it's taking longer than expected. This week's edition is ready for press, so the other staff can cover for me. My article's not due yet, so I can email it in. If I'm delayed into next week, I'll say I caught the flu or something. They won't worry.'

'You never get sick. You're fit and tough as old

boots. They'll never believe it.'

Amy cringed. 'Thanks. I think. Look, we all come and go in the *Gully Standard* office to our own schedule. Trust me, Alex, it's a pretty breezy workplace. Michael and Georgia won't give my absence a second thought.'

Alex shook his head and pushed out a frustrated sigh. 'Amy — '

'I need to do this.' A note of genuine pleading entered her voice. 'For our family. Find out about the real Kelly Bates or whoever she turns out to be. She always spoke proudly of her mother, Alice. Said she was a wonderful strong woman who raised Kelly alone. Her father deserted them and she always seemed angry about that. She said he never had anything to do with them. She said he denied paternity and Alice was completely abandoned.'

'Well before any of that happens, we need to get you out of this freezing tunnel.'

Amy frowned. 'Where are we going?' She hadn't yet found a solution to that question and wondered what he had in mind.

Alex pulled a wry face and shook his head. 'My place.'

His police flat behind the station? Against his professional judgement, he would risk hiding her? On the verge of tears, she mouthed, *Thank you.*

Alex packed up his bag of supplies, slung it over one shoulder and with masterful ease looped an arm around Amy to gently hoist her to her feet. With the warmth from his body pressed against her and the support of his muscled strength, she hobbled slowly toward the pale overcast daylight.

★ ★ ★

Alex shut the tunnel gate entrance again, hoping, unlike some felons, Kelly didn't return to the scene of her crime. At least not for the next few hours. Playing a hunch, there was something he needed to fix first.

To throw Kelly off the scent if she reappeared, it was vital to use the same padlock. Once Amy was safe, he would visit the workshop behind the cottage of local old-timer locksmith Jimmy Webster to repair the padlock Augie had cut to gain entry. It must be replaced. One less problem to deal with if Kelly grew suspicious and decided to check out the tunnel again. Which would create another dilemma, because she would find Amy missing, upping the danger stakes for both sister and Stephen

He settled Amy as comfortably as possible on the back seat of his vehicle and hid her under a blanket. On her instructions, he drove by the cabin for a change of clothes and cash. He hiked upstairs and found them without too much trouble, feeling like a voyeur rummaging in drawers among her bright sexy underwear then sifting through the shelves in her wardrobe for jeans and a sweater.

At the sight of her huge king-sized bed neatly made with a patchwork comforter, he couldn't stop feeling surprised and quietly impressed by the quality of her cosy two-bedroom cabin renovation. That the casual sporty Amy Randall he thought he knew would create her own nest with such homely appeal. Big open fire, comfy sofas and cushions. Rustic kitchen with a generous cooker.

He'd never seen inside her little hideaway home, but then he'd never been invited. No reason to, of course. As Amy said, they were all leading busy lives and usually only ventured a wave and a smile in passing if they met around town.

In future he would make a point of cruising by out here on patrol. Keep an eye on her. After all, she *was* Stephen's baby sister. He would happily do it for his mate. Who he would also now need to keep under close surveillance.

On his way out, Alex found Amy's handbag on the kitchen counter, retrieving her cash and mobile phone. She would need to disable the GPS so she couldn't be tracked. Flick it to aeroplane mode as an extra precaution. Just in case. Since the day he had walked out of Fossicker's Gully fifteen years before, he had learned fast that you never underestimated the enemy.

As he looked over the cabin interior before he closed, checked and locked all doors and windows, he idly wondered if Amy ever got lonely out here. Then he remembered she'd always loved trailing behind him and Stephen, joining in their bush escapades as kids. The girl who made up a trio not feeling like a nuisance. In fact, Alex had always admired her grit and happy spirit.

His mood darkened. To think she had almost been taken away from him. Them. Her family.

After last night's attack, it was his duty now to step up, watch Amy's back and protect Stephen until they knew the extent of Kelly's madness. This next week promised to be a crazy ride, but he would be there for his best mate and his sister, guarding them with his own life and the law.

As he strode back to his car, his professional gut instinct told him Amy should report the attack. That alone would cause upheaval in every Randall life and its fallout erupt among the Gully citizens.

While he understood her reasoning on that front, on the other hand it left an offender loose in their community, even though at this stage it appeared Kelly was primarily a Randall family threat.

He couldn't force Amy to lodge a complaint. Even as the victim, she had the right to stall, but it meant he would need to be doubly vigilant on all fronts.

3

Amy heard the crunch of Alex's boots as he returned to his vehicle, and from beneath the blanket welcomed his muffled reassuring words that all was well and secure in her cabin. Her SUV safely garaged where Kelly left it.

Then she was aware of the short bumpy drive back to his place and the occasional sound of his clicking blinkers as he turned corners. They stopped, a roller door rattled, and they drove through. She heard it lower again. Then as he threw back her covering, she saw true daylight, although dim, for the first time in what she figured must be about seventeen hours. As she had lived it minute by minute, the agonisingly slow passing of time had seemed much longer.

With a steadying hand at her elbow, Alex helped her from his vehicle and hustled her through an interior access door that led directly inside.

Amy released a long sigh. Civilisation again. She hovered on the threshold of his police flat at the rear of the station complex, specially built in recent years. The local Progress and Development Committee had worked hard to make it happen. With old Sergeant Mitchell due to retire, they needed to entice fresh blood into town. Who knew it would be old familiar blood, and exactly what the Gully needed, in the form of one-time rebel Alexander Hammond?

34

As Amy cast her gaze about the almost new modern flat, it occurred to her how basically it was furnished. There were no personal items around, no photographs, no pictures on the walls. Anyone could live here and a guest be none the wiser to their identity. It crossed her mind to wonder why.

It tied in with her impression of a loner, and her heart tugged in empathy for him. That he knew no experience of a close family. Then again, maybe the austere surroundings were just a bloke thing, or he simply wasn't unduly sentimental. Yet the vibes that flowed from him now suggested otherwise. That caring sense of concern, gentler than she remembered, and that strong quiet presence so at odds with his rugged physical presence.

A force to be reckoned with, but from a female viewpoint a body to be admired.

Awkward. She'd never been alone and this close to Alex, like, ever. When that awareness kicked in, even through her shoulder and upper arm's throbbing ache, she grew embarrassingly flustered and felt herself glow.

'You're looking hot.'

If she was feeling a hundred percent, she might take that as a compliment. As it was, Amy merely managed a grin to herself. She knew what he meant, but it could have been taken an entirely different way.

Realising his mistake, Alex looked equally uncomfortable and mumbled, 'You're red-faced, looking feverish.' He stepped closer and placed the back of his big cool hand to her cheeks and forehead. 'The painkillers should help keep any temperature chills at bay.' He paused and scowled. Amy rightly guessed what was coming. 'You know, you really should let me take you to — '

'Absolutely not.' She raised a hand, palm outward toward him. 'If word gets out of the medical centre, the news will spread around town like a summer bushfire with a hot north wind behind it. Kelly can't know I've survived,' she stressed.

Alex confronted her, shaking his head, hands on hips. 'I'm giving you too much rope on this one, Amy. You need to know I don't approve of what you're doing, but I can't force you to report an assault.'

'I know,' she managed in a small voice, although backed with a private confidence and determination, 'and I appreciate your help.'

Perhaps sensing he had been a bit harsh, Alex ran a hand roughly through that gorgeous mop of midnight wavy hair. 'You need to hit a hot shower.' He handed over her bundle of clothes and pointed toward a short hallway. 'Bathroom's that way. Can you manage?'

'I'm good.'

'Okay.' He watched her carefully. 'Then after breakfast, you should catch up on sleep.'

'What I should do and what I intend to do are a different ballgame,' she said wryly, keen to get started on her mission. 'I need to check those records this morning while the library is open.'

'You should lie low for a few days. Give yourself time to recover,' Alex argued, scowling.

His reprimand made her feel like she was a schoolgirl again, and a burden tagging along behind Stephen and his best mate all those years ago.

'I don't have time,' she protested, mumbling, 'I'll try not to be a nuisance.'

He shrugged and said simply, 'You've never been that.'

Reflecting on her childhood forays with the boys, Amy was surprised to hear it. Her sometimes pleading requests had often been answered with groans from Stephen and glaring-eyed silence from Alex. Being the lost tomboy sister, he left approval to the big brother. Who mostly reluctantly agreed.

She had idolised Alex with that edge of danger about him, those dark flashing eyes always vigilant. His nature now not so much subdued as mellowed. Once resistant to authority and the law, he now upheld it. But while she had admired her brother's best mate from afar, it had always been clearly understood that the Randall and Hammond worlds were never likely to intersect.

Amy padded down the hall, nosily peering aside at two bedrooms along the way. One clearly an office, the other military-neat and spare. Impressive. And like hers, dominated by a king-sized bed. Made sense. They were both tall people.

She closed the bathroom door, aware Alex was only metres away, then turned on the shower and slowly undressed. Muscle stiffness from her wound and overnight exposure to cold were setting in, but the hot water streaming over her body soon thawed and revived.

Towelled dry and tingling, she pulled on her stretch jeans and long jumper, wandering out to the living area again to join Alex, refreshed.

And find he had cooked breakfast. Softly scrambled eggs on toast sprinkled with herbs, just the way she liked it. How could he know? Coincidence? They had camped out in the reserve plenty of times as kids and cooked food over an open fire, but surely Alex wouldn't remember from all those years ago? Maybe he had one of those photographic memories.

Ah. She mentally pulled herself up. Too much overthinking for this early in the day. She needed to save her brain for research.

'Thanks,' she mumbled as he placed the steaming hot food before her.

'Tea?' he asked. She nodded and he obliged. 'I'll hit the shower. Enjoy,' he murmured.

While Alex prepared for work, despite her creaking body and weariness from her overnight trauma, Amy found enough of an appetite to gratefully eat most of what he had prepared.

He returned dressed in uniform. Amy had seen him from a distance around town, of course, looking all official in his police gear. But now, close up, he set her pulse racing, and it wasn't from the shock and aftermath of what she had endured last night.

He was one sexy dude.

Navy-blue cargo pants, long-sleeved shirt. He draped his police cap, black boots and equipment belt over a lounge chair and joined her for a quick breakfast. She should feel guilty for making him pushed for time, but Amy privately sighed with pleasure watching him eat as she nursed her mug of tea.

Between shovelling in mouthfuls of cereal from a bowl standing against a kitchen cupboard while Amy snuggled up on his sofa across the room, Alex said, 'A young local guy asked me to keep an eye on his vehicle while's he's overseas for a month. It's white and small and insignificant. I'll go get it and park it out the back of the station for you. It's private down here at the end of the main street and won't attract much traffic or attention.'

He had spoken, dumped his empty dish in the sink and disappeared before Amy had barely opened her mouth. As the door closed, she whispered, 'Thank you,' stunned by the gesture and his foresight.

Within ten minutes, she heard a vehicle return. Alex reappeared and handed Amy the keys. As their hands touched in the changeover, a sense of intimacy spiked through her.

She pulled away and wrapped her fingers around the keys. 'Alex, I'm super grateful for this.'

He shrugged his big shoulders and his shirt stretched across his body. 'You're welcome. If anyone asks why the car's here, I'll just say I figured it was safer where I can keep an eye on it. While I'm on my rounds and out on patrol this morning, I'll call in on Stephen at the youth club and hint about your *absence*.' He grinned.

Amy remained blown away by the extent of his

generosity. He was really on board and getting involved in this whole deal. She hoped nothing backfired and there was no need for regret. When all this was over, she owed him. Big time.

'Thanks. He'll pass on the information to Kelly. They share everything.' She restlessly paced the living room and nervously twisted her hands together. 'I should warn him, Alex. He's living with a murderer!'

'I know,' he said softly, sensitive to her anguish, striding across the room to place an arm carefully on her good shoulder, his hand drifting higher to massage the back of neck beneath her fall of damp dark hair.

If she had been a cat, she would have purred. Alex's touch was hypnotic. So when he moved away, she immediately felt deprived and that old familiar longing returned with a vengeance. Damn.

Alex suggested, 'Use your phone camera to record anything you feel might prove useful to your case.'

'Sure.'

'From here on in, you need every scrap of evidence you can find. No matter how small it seems.'

They air-dropped each other's mobile numbers.

Alex studied her silently for a while. 'What if you strike trouble?' he murmured, worry lines wrinkling his forehead.

Such humble sweetness from a big strapping guy made him appear cute and vulnerable. 'From doing a little research? I doubt that.'

'Ames,' he said, using her childhood nick-name, 'everyone in town knows your face, and Kelly's tried to bump you off once already. If she discovers you're still alive ... ' He shook his head.

'She won't.'

'She lives two blocks away,' he tossed back, frustrated.

Where had the cool-headed cop suddenly gone? Alex Hammond, caring? 'I'll be fine. Don't worry.'

He planted big hands on his hips, looking dangerous and gorgeous at the same time. 'I've always worried about you,' he admitted quietly.

'You have?' Amy paused, gobsmacked by his admission, her heart beating just a tad faster again. 'You and my brother were always off on your adventures. Even if I was allowed to join you, I thought you barely knew I existed.'

'You were a hard girl — and now woman — to ignore.'

'I was?' she said wryly. 'I am?'

'I didn't mean being so stubborn. More that you're . . . appealing. In your own way,' he drawled.

'Well I'll take that as your first compliment ever.'

She made light of the direction the conversation was taking, but in her heart of hearts, she felt something primal stir. From their banter, was he hinting that her feelings just might be returned? Was that even possible? Something to explore another time, perhaps.

'Yeah.' He grinned. 'Sorry it's a bit late.'

'Oh, it's never too late to hear some positive personal praise,' she said brightly, trying to be casual.

As a distraction from the growing air of tension in the room, Amy scrambled for her phone and cash, stuffing both into her pockets. She pushed her hair up under the beanie part-disguise Alex offered before he strapped on his police equipment belt. She longed for sleep but would only allow herself that luxury later.

Trying to appear more agile than she felt with Alex watching, Amy slid carefully into the small borrowed car, cringed as she clicked on her seatbelt, turned the key, and put it in gear. She gave him a false smile of confidence and a thumbs-up. Pushing past her physical discomfort, she caught one last glimpse of him in her rear-view mirror before slinking as low as possible in her seat, but still high enough to see over the windscreen, as she drove away.

★　★　★

After Amy left, Alex opened up the station and dealt with a few early concerned phone calls and minor issues from the public. When it grew quiet, he closed up and headed for the youth club, where he knew Stephen would be both playing and coaching badminton.

His mate was a creature of habit. Regular as clockwork in work and play, like his monthly scheduled sports pistol shoot this afternoon. It flashed to mind that at least a licenced firearm owner wasn't responsible for its illegal use in a

42

homicide, so no blame would fall on his mate. Being in the company office all day anyway, he had a cast-iron alibi. It wasn't unusual for Alex Hammond, on duty or off, to drop by these youth mornings, so his uniformed presence wouldn't raise any alarms. But knowing the truth about his mate's wife now, he still felt like he had been punched in the gut when he caught sight of Stephen.

With life's experience and in his police work, Alex usually managed to hold back, but today it was going to take all of his self-control not to blab the truth about Kelly. Especially since Amy had already been attacked and, by association, Stephen's personal safety was threatened, too.

It was a horrid secret to keep until Amy consented to press charges. Alex hated the delay but understood her need to dig deeper into Kelly's background. Personally, Alex thought Amy was living dangerously by not reporting the incident, and she had a bullet wound in her shoulder to prove it. He felt helpless with Amy away on her own and Kelly still on the loose. He neither liked nor approved of the whole damned nasty situation.

Alex waved in greeting as Stephen jogged over. 'Can't stay long, mate. Just wanted to catch you. Saw Amy late yesterday heading home before taking off on assignment for the *Standard*. Said to let you know she would be away for a few days.'

'Yeah, she mentioned the article. Some special feature piece.' Stephen frowned. 'Thought that wasn't for a few weeks yet.'

Alex shrugged. 'She seemed keen to get away over the weekend to make a start.'

'Where's she gone?'

Alex cringed before he lied. 'Good question. She didn't say and I didn't ask. I know — ' He grinned sheepishly. ' — me not grilling people, right?'

Even as the irony crossed his mind, he knew he was about to do that exact thing, and for the first time in life that he could recall, having to choose between brother and sister.

Through the mysterious laws of compatibility between an angry man from across the railway line on the wrong side of town and the biggest businessman in Fossicker's Gully and mayor's son, somehow moody Alex Hammond and handsome Stephen Randall had been friends since boyhood.

Their mateship ran deep and loyal, so he felt devious and found it hard facing the man for what Amy had asked of him and he now felt obliged to do. But after last night's attempted murder, it had become vitally important he try and find out about his friend's home life and relationship with his wife.

'So, how's Kelly and everything at home?'

Stephen flashed him a quick sideways glance. 'Fine, of course. Why are you asking?'

'I don't have much of a role model in my own family. I admire yours. The Randalls have always been stable and reputable in the community, and highly regarded, especially in business.'

Stephen hesitated and lowered his voice. 'When does your old man get out?'

44

'Soon. That's one of the reasons why I came back. Watch out for Mum. Make sure she's safe. Buddy's heading down the same bad road as our father. Got no proof yet, but I think he's into something dodgy. Easy money.'

'Bud's been working for us, driving trucks, for two years now. Foreman's had to give him a nudge now and then to keep his logbook on track. You know we have strict driver rules for work and rest periods.'

'Sure do. Keep onto Buddy, mate. I appreciate you even giving him a job after his last conviction.'

'We're in the process of installing a live fleet tracking system. Identify poor driving to improve behaviour and safety. It will give us information on speeding, hard braking and stuff to understand how the fleet's being driven. If any driver needs further education,' he said pointedly, 'the company will pay for it.'

'Glad to hear it. As the second oldest, Buddy's been Jim's favourite, since I wouldn't get involved in any of the old man's shady schemes. He focused on turning Bud to learning about quick bucks, which means getting involved with tough types. I don't want our youngest brother Billy going down that same road. See a lot of myself in him at that age. He's angry like I used to be. Needs a firm hand, support and steering straight.'

'Sorry you've got trouble brewing on the home front, mate. Makes me grateful for my own decent wife and marriage and being raised in an upright family.'

45

Even as he walked away, Alex was this close to turning back and spitting out the truth about Kelly, sick in the gut to hear a guy sound so happy, blind to being fooled and having no idea his world was about to crash.

Shit, he could barely look his friend in the face. Personally, he'd like to plant his hands firmly around his mate's wife's pretty little neck and squeeze.

And although Stephen thought his family was perfect, rumours had been floating around for years about his father David Randall's loose hands around women. Alex wondered if his wife Cora was suspicious or would even admit she knew of her husband's poor reputation. Possible but unlikely, although sometimes the spouse *was* the last to know.

Growing up, Stephen had never hinted at suspecting anything. Back then, Amy had been in the background of his mateship with her brother. The kid sister was all attitude and long awkward legs like a filly finding her feet.

Maybe now that she had turned to him last night for help, he'd get to know her better. Hard not to notice that those gangly legs had filled out nice and shapely. Damn mystery why no man in town had claimed her. Maybe her independent streak kept them distant, but he'd seen a softer, vulnerable side in the tunnel. She had confided, been strong despite her serious injury, and bravely played down her level of pain.

Now she was set on going out seeking answers to protect her brother and their family. Although nothing justified any criminal act, especially

46

attempted murder. Alex just hoped Amy found an explanation behind Kelly's actions yesterday before someone else got hurt. He'd be keeping a close eye on Kelly and watching Stephen's back for sure.

And both as a friend and also as a policeman, he was more than happy to give his support to Amy until the mess was resolved.

4

As Amy had driven away from the police house, she kept to the back streets of Fossicker's Gully to avoid people and get out of town unnoticed, made slightly easier by the fact that it was still early and most people were enjoying starting slow on their Saturday morning.

Then it had only been a forty-minute run through flat grazing countryside, on gently winding roads edged with straggly gums into the bustling country town of her destination, Maryborough. Suffering the rawness of her injury, Amy was grateful to be familiar with the local roads and light traffic, taking it steady.

The country city still retained its grand old historic buildings like the town hall and courthouse, plus the ornate red-brick railway station. Its narrow streetscapes were historic with verandas, the post office and clock tower, beautiful Princes Park public gardens and Lake Victoria.

At the Resource Centre, Amy pulled in as far as possible toward the back of the car park so her borrowed vehicle was not easily seen or noticed. Not from paranoia or the expectation of being found by Kelly, but Alex had expressed acute concern for her safety, so she decided to take the small extra precaution.

Inside the building with its huge glass front, Amy's focus was not the visitor information centre but the regional library with public computers. Her concealment was vital while she sorted out the cause of Kelly's alarming actions yesterday.

As Amy began searching genealogy records and scanning the pages of old newspaper records now digitised online, she was constantly distracted by her ongoing aching body and deep sapping weariness. She took a brief break for a coffee, but even as she continued, was frustrated not to find the Alice Bates she sought.

Hours later, Amy's usual patience crumbled in the wake of total defeat when her research bombed. Everywhere she looked, no Alice Bates existed. Even in the voters' rolls. Birth records, she discovered, were unavailable under government privacy laws if the person was still living or born less than a hundred years ago.

Since Kelly said her mother had apparently died in recent years, that meant death record limitations beyond the 1980s were also no help. Even with the assistance of an obliging lady genealogist on duty who explained the restrictions on information available and other possible avenues for Amy to investigate, she came up empty.

The possibility of success via online cemetery indexes, family trees and genealogy organisations had her hopes briefly raised, but again, to no avail. Nothing. As if *her* Alice Bates was a ghost. Which, by late morning, Amy was growing to believe might be more true than funny. If Kelly would stoop to murder, had she also lied about her mother's identity?

The irony was, most of the websites she searched were readily available, and she could have stayed back at the police house in the Gully and done her research in comfort on Alex's laptop without all this extra effort.

Before she collapsed and fell asleep over the computer terminal keyboard, around noon Amy decided to call it quits and head home. Well, at least back to her hometown and Alex. Stimulating thought. Even more motivating was the thought of a few hours of sorely needed sleep.

★ ★ ★

After leaving Stephen at the youth club late morning, Alex cruised the town, making sure his patch and its people were safe and their lives peaceful. Often the reason local residents lived in the country, having been born in town and staying, never feeling the need to leave. Or tree changers escaping the city, soon enough being welcomed and becoming part of the small-town community.

The main street on this Saturday morning looked normal, but there would be the odd overindulgence in alcohol tonight and into the early hours, especially celebrating a win or loss at the local football oval. The Gully Demons were playing the Ironbark Tigers today on their home ground. Ironbark, once a nearby thriving small town, was now nothing more than a cluster of ramshackle houses you passed on your way through to somewhere else.

With the Demons and the Tigers being among

the top teams in the competition, it promised to be a close match. He would swing by later to mingle with the crowd at the recreation reserve, and keep an eye on the usual handful of suspects whose harmless fun often tended to edge toward unruly.

Turning away from the central part of town, Alex found himself driving by his parents' rundown house. An old compact weatherboard Jim and Selma had lived in all their married life and eventually owned thanks to his mother's dogged hard work to pay it off. Head held high and working class, Selma Hammond was the family's role model.

The neglected house saw little maintenance or paint. Selma didn't have time, not yet sixty but looking older, and Jim was too lazy for honest work. With its weedy yard and looking unloved, Selma at least managed to keep the inside clean. In years past, three bedrooms meant all the kids doubled up for sleeping. Alex stuck with Buddy until he left home.

Only Billy lived with their mother under its rusty roof these days, and Jim when he was out. Which wasn't often. Prison had become a revolving door for the petty criminal Alex was ashamed to know as his father.

Jim was still locked up, of course, but Selma would be working, as was her habit, pretty much seven days a week if she could grab the hours. Cleaning private homes and motels in town, cooking in the pub kitchen. There was no vehicle in the driveway. Never had been. His family couldn't afford one. Selma rode a bicycle everywhere. Jim walked.

Alex's deepest enduring wish was to get Selma away from this domestic shambles. It surely had never been a home. That way, at least his mother could finally know peace in her life. After decades of poverty and abuse, she deserved it.

On the day Jim had been sent to prison again, twelve months before, Selma had made her own quiet prediction. 'He'll always end up back there. Can't help himself. Don't learn from his mistakes.'

Most prisoners were younger than his old man and likely to have been inside before. Even though Victorian prisons were mostly regional and Jim was currently in Loddon at Castlemaine, Selma never visited him.

The last time he was sentenced and admitted, Alex had pleaded for her to leave him.

Selma had gently laid a hand on her oldest son's arm, a resigned look on her face. 'You know I'll be stayin'. I got nowhere else to go. This place has become a habit.' Her lined mouth had edged into a grin and she leaned closer. 'Besides, he's not always here, is he?' She chuckled.

'I can get you newer and more comfortable public housing accommodation,' Alex had urged.

'I don't have the energy to start again, son. I know you mean well, and you're a good man, but I don't need much. I'm comfortable enough right here.'

'After all these years, I understand change is confrontational, but you'd just be moving on, simple as that. Still here in Fossicker's Gully with your work. Julie and I will be here for you.' He sighed. 'When Lisa wises up and realises she's worthy of more respect from her deadbeat partner, she'll probably join you.'

Selma had shaken her head and muttered, 'That man of hers is no damn good.'

At the time of that conversation with his mother, Alex had backed off. But so help him, if his father so much as raised a finger in his mother's direction when he got out soon, he would pounce.

Now, eyeing off the humble dwelling that screamed for either demolition or a makeover, Alex despaired anew. He helped where he could, but his mother was so damned independent and proud, he only occasionally managed to bypass her strict permission. A day's gardener here, a handyman there. Inside was dated but neat and tidy. When his mother was home, the tempting smells from her kitchen were mind-blowing. He sometimes wondered if her cooking was a source of contentment.

Billy still lived at home but went missing from time to time. AWOL from school, which made Alex angry because his kid brother was smart with his hands. If he was prepared to knuckle down, he could really make something of his life. They were the reasons he had returned to his hometown. It didn't have much, but it had his family and memories. Not all good, for sure, but enough to entice him back.

And now there was Amy Randall in the mix. Funny how life turned out and brought a detour when you least expected it.

As Alex steered his vehicle out of his old home street and around the corner, he noticed trouble up ahead. A huddle of young men, aimless and begging for trouble, being a nuisance and causing disruption. He drew closer and pulled up at the local family park and playground, recognising every one of them — his brother Billy among them, he was annoyed to see. Being rough with playground equipment, disturbing and frightening mothers and children, babies in prams.

As he left the police vehicle, put on his cap and approached them, Alex knew the best solution was dispersal. Striding with easy authority across the grass, he nodded to the mothers, who gathered their children and moved away.

Standing astride, arms folded, Alex addressed each lad by name, followed by a short conversation, basically a warning with a threat to involve their parents next time and press charges, while suggesting they all split up and move on.

'William Hammond,' he said with a scowl at his brother, 'you know better.' He pointed towards the police cruiser. 'Hop in.'

'I can walk.'

'I said hop in. Right now, I'm not your big brother. I'm in uniform, I have a job to do, and this is official business, understand? You disobey me and it's another offence. I've let you off lightly today but don't push it.' Alex's voice was hard, his attitude serious, and Billy knew it. 'We need to talk.'

Alex watched his brother's hunched shoulders

of annoyance as he walked back across the park to his vehicle, while he had a quiet word of apology and reassurance to the mothers and their families watching from the sidelines. Any one of them could have been his sister Lisa and little niece Gracie.

Alex joined Billy and started up the vehicle, driving slowly to the edge of town and pulling up in a roadside layby with a picnic table beneath gum trees. The air between the brothers was tense, with no conversation since leaving the park. Alex wound down the car windows and cut the engine.

'So what did you think you were achieving back there?'

With narrowed eyes and an expression of defiance across his face, Billy looked away from his policeman brother and out the passenger window. 'I was just watching.'

'You were an accomplice to misdemeanours with the potential to be charged with damaging public property.'

'I didn't do anything.'

'Exactly. You were loitering. Not doing anything. You should be studying or working at a job.'

'What's the point?'

Alex heard the despair in the kid's voice and remembered the same sense of hopelessness from his own youth. The reason he lit out as soon as he could.

'The point is,' Alex murmured slow, determined not to lecture, but be an ear, a listener, and to give the lad encouragement, 'you knew those boys were doing wrong, yet even more gutlessly, you just sat by and watched, laughing. You think that's so wise now?' Silence. 'There were young mothers with children in that park. What if Lisa and Gracie had been there? Would you have been happy to act tough and threaten them, too?'

'No.'

'Then why believe it's acceptable for anyone else?'

Again, no response, just sullen tension thick around them. Alex sighed to himself. Some young folk found an interest like a part-time job or sport, but Billy seemed to be falling through the cracks. You'd think he would have the perfect role model for hard work in their own mother.

'A word of advice, Billy. You need to forget where you came from and make your own life. I did.'

'You left,' his young brother accused with a level of bitterness Alex completely understood.

Billy thought he'd been abandoned. Alex had always watched out for him as a kid. He was the youngest and most defenceless.

'Yep. Got out as quick as I could but I finished high school first,' he snuck in a hint based on Billy's known bouts of truancy this year, 'but somehow I always knew I'd come back.' He turned reflective.

'Why?'

At the time, Alex hadn't known himself, but over the years he learned. 'Because somehow I wanted to make a difference. Had no idea how. I just felt a growing need to help people. Keep 'em straight. Especially the young and vulnerable. Women. Kids. Young folk who needed steering in the right direction and a quiet word of encouragement or praise. Something we sure didn't get from our old man. Jim is no role model or example to anyone. Do you want to give up now before your life has started and end up like him?'

'Ma works hard.'

'She surely does.' Alex nodded in acknowledgement, heartened that it seemed Billy had at least been listening and felt more comfortable joining in the conversation, his defences lowered. Maybe he could get through to the boy after all. 'She's a strong reason why I came back. To check on her and my brothers and sisters.'

'Even Buddy?' Billy scoffed in disbelief.

'Yep, even him.' Alex paused and said in a softer brotherly tone, 'I know you were knocked around and treated hard by our alcoholic father, but I watched out for you as long as I could. There were nine years between you and me and three siblings in between. I knew I'd never get ahead in life if I stayed till you were older. I had to trust you'd be okay, and I can tell you, Billy, even to this day despite all I've seen and done in my life, walking out of town the day I finished school was still the hardest thing I ever did.'

'I hated you,' Billy said quietly through gritted teeth.

Alex was willing to bet he was fighting back tears, but didn't glance in his direction and cause embarrassment. 'Not surprised. But I kept in touch. Ma pass that on?'

Billy nodded.

'Sounds like Buddy's been foxy while working for Randall Transport, but Stephen's on to him and bringing in checking systems and stricter rules. Lisa's heading for trouble if she stays with Mick. You and Julie are the youngest but both have potential. She's ambitious to succeed in her own business, and at the moment, the world is your oyster, Billy. You know you have skills, you just need to finish school and use them.'

'I don't have any money.'

'That the case. Well if you don't get out and earn it, you'll never have any. You were only nine when I left, but in the years before that, can you remember what I did?'

Billy shrugged. 'Jobs and stuff.'

'I pounded the pavement up and down Main Street, in and out of every business, begging for work. Offered to do anything, didn't care what so long as it paid me something and was honest money. First thing I did was save for a bike and paid cash. Beat walking, even in a small town like the Gully. Saved for driving lessons and got that.'

'So you're Mr. Wonderful. I get it.' Billy grew resentful.

'I didn't tell you to brag. I hope you know me better than that. Don't be smart and don't be jealous. First thing you need to do is get stubborn and mean business. Have a plan. Something you want real bad, and go for it. Don't let anyone talk you out of it or tell you it can't be done. Because I'm proof it can. And don't confide your dream to anyone. Especially those larrikins you hang with.'

He turned to his brother and urged with meaning, 'What do you want, Billy?' He gave him a moment, then went on, 'I wanted to see what was outside Fossicker's Gully, what people did, how they lived, how it might be different to my life. Simply wanted to know what else was out there. Nothing specific, just that I wanted something better for me.'

Alex lowered his voice. 'I had no help from anyone, either. Jim was useless, and Ma had her hands full raising us kids and working herself ragged so we could eat, providing for her family where our father failed. You respect that woman, Billy. *She's* the example to follow. Quietly getting stuff done and never complaining. You're still living at home, so you watch out for her. When Jim gets out, if he raises a hand to her, you stand up to him for the weak man he is. Get between him and your mother, or you come and get me. Either as your brother or Sergeant Hammond. Your choice.

'You're almost eighteen, Billy. Time enough now to start growing up, making decent decisions. Protecting those you love, and respecting women. Your sisters, too. Julie wants to own that hair salon one day. She's saving to buy it out when Gwen retires in a few years. And she's choosy about the guys she dates. Makes sure they treat her right and control their drink. You got a role model in her, too. See much of Lisa?'

Billy shrugged. 'Some. She's unhappy with

59

Mick. Little Gracie's cute.'

'Lisa's wary of me now because I wear a uniform, so I try and visit when I'm off duty. But she gets defensive. When we chat, I make no secret that I know she can do better than the man she chose. Mick's got work, but he spends too much money on cars and time with his mates instead of being there for his woman and child. They're both vulnerable. She's probably fed up with me telling her to aim for something, too. Improve her situation. Get work outside the house or study. Ma doesn't have much free time working like she does, but she loves kids, is a caring grandmother to her one and only, and I'll bet if Lisa asked she'd mind little Gracie a few hours now and then.

'Only way to stop the cycle of life is to man up and help others to do the same. Kindness and manners don't cost a cent.'

'How do I know where to start?' Billy asked in a small voice.

'Get thinking. Roll a few ideas around in your mind. You can keep whingeing or do something to make the change. Up to you. Be interested to hear what you decide.'

The police radio crackled into life with an official duty call. Alex responded, noting details.

He hung up and sighed. 'Sorry, mate. You heard. Sounds like old Eddie Ryan is involved in an accident out at The Junction again.' A web of country roads that formed a tricky intersection the local government region had been fighting for years to acquire funding to fix. 'You're gonna have to get out of the car. I need to go straight to the scene. Only a kilometre back into town. Do you mind?'

'Course I do,' Billy snapped, glowering.

Alex grinned to himself as his kid brother stepped out of the vehicle and slammed the door. 'Think positive,' he called out through his open window. 'You can use the walk for thinking of your plan and to work off some of that anger at me.'

As he belted up and flicked on his blinker, Alex checked in his rear-view mirror to make sure Billy was heading toward the Gully before speeding away. The boy's shoulders were slumped, hands thrust into the pockets of his baggy jeans. He looked younger than eighteen. Raised tough like all the Hammond kids but still vulnerable. Yet, judging by Billy's spark of attention this morning, he was beginning to hold out hope for the young man.

★ ★ ★

After being at the youth club all morning, Stephen Randall shut the impressive double front doors of his home and dumped his sports gear in the hall, keen to clean up after a physical workout with the kids, grab the prepared sandwich Kelly would have ready for him to eat on the way and drive to his monthly shooting meet in Trentham.

Although a waiting Kelly smiled at him, an air of censure laced her greeting. 'You're later than usual, my love. No trouble with any of the young people at the club?'

61

'No. Just ran into Alex Hammond and chatted for a while. He was out on patrol but called in to let me know Amy's out of town for a few days.'

'Oh?'

His wife's expression sharpened. Her attention didn't usually peak with such interest and surprise on the rare occasion he dared mention his sister. It hurt him that friction had always existed between the two women. Odd, because Kelly was so sweet, and Amy's easygoing nature meant she could normally fit in with anyone. He often wondered if it was simply sibling jealousy.

'Yeah. Some assignment for a special article in the *Standard*.'

'When did he see her?'

Stephen shrugged. 'Yesterday on her way home from work, apparently. Last-minute decision. You know Amy.' He smiled fondly.

As Stephen went to shower and change, Kelly Randall paced around her townhouse preening, a smug smile on her perfectly made-up face. This news couldn't be better. She most certainly had nothing to worry about now. It was enough that Amy's absence wouldn't have been noticed when she didn't show up for work on Monday morning, but this? She resisted laughing to herself in case Stephen overheard.

No one would be looking for her sister-in-law or raising any alarm until well into next week. She could relax. She was safe. The wounded woman's exposure for so long in that icy tunnel meant certain death. Hypothermia would set in and nature would take care of the rest.

Ten minutes later, she experienced a moment

of alarm when Stephen reappeared, carrying his pistol case, and fondly teased her on his way out.

'You been cleaning my gun cupboard again?'

Kelly pretended genuine contrition, using the humble voice that always worked on her husband. 'It was looking dusty. You don't mind?'

'Course not,' he murmured, kissing her warmly. 'Just noticed my pistol slightly out of place.'

Kelly chastised herself for the rare and unacceptable blunder. 'Apologies, my love. I thought rack of lamb tonight?' she said quickly in distraction, deferring to her husband's decision. But dinner was already planned and she knew he would agree.

Stephen grinned. 'Perfect. Be back around six.'

5

Amy sped back along the road to Fossicker's Gully around midday, the dull grey autumn weather filled with the dampness of the previous night's heavy rain when she had been stuck in an old mine tunnel fearing for her survival.

It all seemed like a nightmare now at the hands of her sister-in-law. Her shoulder wound ached a treat, and she barely managed to keep her eyes open even on the short drive back.

As she approached the edge of town, she slunk low in her vehicle. Once again she avoided the main street, eventually pulling into the back of the police station. Alex's patrol car was missing, so he must still be out on duty. The station would be locked but she hoped the house wasn't.

Keeping low behind the property fence, Amy crept to the back door and tried the knob. It rattled but wouldn't open. Damn. And she didn't figure Alex would be a soul to keep his house key under the mat or a pot plant. All the same, she searched. Nothing.

She was just wondering how long she would have to wait when her phone rang. She glanced at her mobile screen. The object of her thoughts. 'Alex. Great timing. I'm stuck at your back door.'

'Yeah, sorry about that.'

'Where are you?'

'Five minutes away. Had to attend a road accident.'

'Feel free to break the speed limit,' she quipped, sliding to sit on the coir mat backed up against the wall.

★ ★ ★

Alex turned the corner into Main Street, intending to head straight for the station to rescue Amy from lockout at his place. Until a young guy jogged across the road alongside and rapped on his driver's-side window while the vehicle was still moving.

Alex braked and pulled into an angle park. 'Everything okay, mate?' he asked the young man as he eased from the car and stood to greet him.

'I think Charlie's car's been stolen.'

Alex's attention snapped to alert and he ran a weary hand over his face and down the back of his neck. 'Right. When did you see it?'

'Just now.' The young guy was antsy. 'Young chick driving.' He frowned. 'You know, I reckon she looked familiar, but I mean, a local girl wouldn't steal a car and then go driving it around town right under everyone's noses, right?'

'You wouldn't think so.' Alex winced and asked in an official voice, 'Description?'

'Small white VW Golf. Isn't worth much, but Charlie relies on it, and — '

Alex raised a hand to stall his gushing and tendered his most confident policeman smile.

65

'It's okay. Charlie asked me to keep an eye on it.'

'Then what's it doing on the road when you're in this?' He pointed to the police car alongside.

'I need you to work with me here, mate. Charlie's a young friend we both clearly know. In my case from a couple minor offences of a weekend,' he hinted.

'We all like a beer on a Saturday night,' the young man scoffed.

'Sure. Understand that, mate. But Charlie asked me to keep an eye on his vehicle, which I'm doing. Could have left it exposed in the carport at his flat, but I figured it was safer at the station where I can keep an eye on it. The young woman in question you saw driving the VW today is of excellent character in a spot of bother at the moment, a person who needs support right now. And privacy, if you get my meaning?'

The young man shrugged. 'If you say so.'

Alex ignored the attitude and placed a hand companionably on the guy's shoulder. 'The woman needed to make a short trip while I was on duty attending a single vehicle accident on the road. As you saw, Charlie's car is back now, and the vehicle is safe and sound. But good job on a keen eye in the community, though. That's what small towns are about. Everyone looking out for each other. Appreciate your diplomacy to keep that in mind and this conversation between us.'

'Sure.'

'I hear Charlie's backpacking around Europe. Heard from him?' Alex asked, edging the conversation away from the car.

'Yeah. Somewhere in Spain, I think.'

'Great. Heading down to the footy this afternoon?'

'Sure am.'

Alex smiled. 'Then enjoy the rest of your day.'

'Thanks, Sergeant.'

★ ★ ★

Alex returned later than promised, during which time, to Amy's embarrassment, she fought to keep her eyes open, but must have dozed off because she woke to Alex gently shaking her.

'Hey, Sleeping Beauty.'

'That was a long five minutes,' she muttered, struggling to stand, Alex whipping a strong hand under her elbow to help her rise.

Amy yawned and dragged off her beanie, mussing her tumble of shoulder-length dark hair. Alex unlocked the door and stepped aside to let her pass. As she finally entered his domain, Amy pushed out a long sigh of stored tension and exhaustion she hadn't realised she was holding in.

She'd done it. She was safe.

Then as Alex closed the door behind them, he completely sent her relaxation into a spin again. 'You've been seen. You're going to have to be more careful.'

Amy's heart thumped in shock. 'By Kelly?'

'No. A mate of Charlie's recognised the car.'

She groaned. 'Really? What are the odds?'

Alex grinned. 'It's okay. I managed to explain

and reassure him. But it might be best if you lie low.'

'It's okay.' Amy covered her mouth as she yawned again. 'I've discovered I can do most research online on any laptop, but I might still need to get around. You'll be pleased to hear that, for now though, I'm not planning on moving an inch.' She moved toward his comfy sofa. 'Because I need to sleep.'

'How about I duck out to the bakery and get some meat pies for lunch? Then you can bunk down in my bed when I go out again.'

The thought of that big beautiful bed all to herself, and that Alex usually slept in it, made Amy almost blush.

'You sure?' she squeaked, hoping he didn't change his mind.

'Positive. Stay awake long enough to eat, then my bedroom's all yours.'

Except Alex wouldn't be in it. But she would manage. Amy knew from personal experience that a girl could live on dreams. For years.

★ ★ ★

Within fifteen minutes, the pies were eaten, Alex remade his bed just for her — handsome *and* a domestic god? — then tactfully disappeared into the police station. Amy stripped to her underwear and T-shirt, then spread out her long limbs to snuggle beneath his doona and rest her head on one of his pillows.

Her last thoughts as she heard light rain on the roof were that the poor footballers would be playing in the mud and she hoped the Demons won.

When Amy stirred, the room was just as dull as when she went to sleep, but she felt way better. She used all the bed in a luxurious stretch, pushed off the doona and rose. She needed to pee. She was urgently striding head down halfway to the bathroom when she slammed into Alex.

Amy froze. Nothing she could do in the situation, half dressed, a pair of appreciative brown eyes flashing all over her like lightning. Her body responded by flooding warm and hot, then chilled with embarrassment at her exposure.

Not knowing what else to do, she made light of the situation, raised her hands and quipped, 'I'm not armed, Sergeant.'

'Doesn't mean you're not dangerous,' he drawled. 'I should change that dressing on your arm again,' he murmured as he swivelled on his polished black boots and retreated.

Amy entertained a few wicked thoughts of her own but kept her mouth shut. As she used the bathroom, she marvelled that worldly Alex had looked equally uncomfortable at their sudden encounter. But not disappointed? That flicker of his eyebrows and threatening grin which he hadn't let loose speaking volumes.

Amy dressed, combed fingers through her hair for a quick tidy, and went to face her policeman. She believed in facing down demons. Getting it over with would clear the air.

As she entered the living area, Alex turned

from the kitchen. 'Sorry. Should have knocked or made a noise or something. You were so whacked when I left, I thought you'd still be sleeping.'

'Alex, you're thirty. I'm sure you've encountered a few ladies in bikinis in your travels. Or even less,' she teased, chuckling.

'Right.'

'I seem to survive on a few hours' sleep,' she explained. 'I feel great.'

The steady gaze from his dark eyes hinted that maybe she *looked* great, too. Flustered, Amy went on quickly, 'Who won the footy?'

'We did.'

'Yay. Be a busy night in town for you, then.'

'Ben Jordan, our local security officer, has agreed to patrol town on his usual rounds while I take a dinner break in about an hour. He'll contact me if there's any trouble, but I'll need to head back out later. From memory, you pretty much eat anything, right?'

He was doing a lot of remembering lately, Amy noted. Just nostalgia like her, or something more? 'Sure.'

'Fish and chips or Chinese?'

'I love Asian.'

'Me too. Any favourites?'

She shook her head. 'Surprise me.'

'I think I already did,' he mumbled with a frisky grin, 'but after Kelly, that's a challenge.'

Delighted by his humour, she laughed. 'Okay, I could go for a curry.'

'Spicy it is,' he drawled.

Amy dug her hands into her jeans pockets and shrugged. 'After all you've done, I'd offer to pay, but I have limited cash for emergencies and I can't use my credit card.'

'Not a problem. My treat.'

The door clicked shut as he left.

Amy fanned herself and gaped. What was that all about? Hammond flirting? And that dry sense of humour? Where had he been keeping that hidden? This was a laid-back side of the man she'd known all her life but never seen. She found herself looking forward to his return, if only to see what happened next.

★ ★ ★

True to his word, Alex was back in sixty-five minutes. Living with newspaper deadlines, Amy had instinctively checked her watch.

It was great to have company again, especially the security of the local cop, but Amy's reason for joy and relief was her growing restless energy. With a few hours' sleep, her mind buzzed again, and she was edgy to start getting answers to the Kelly mystery. So far she had turned up zilch, and it was driving her nuts.

Since Alex left, she had paced the flat and chewed over possible scenarios. One in particular could be carried out in the morning, but she needed to run her idea past him first.

'Smells wonderful.' She smiled as he entered and dumped the containers on the kitchen bench, removing his navy-blue cap, operations vest and equipment belt.

'Chopsticks?' He produced two sets from a drawer.

71

Amy shook her head and pulled a wry face. 'Never got the knack.'

Alex chuckled. 'When I was in remote Asia, it was either get the hang of them, use your fingers, or starve.'

He handed her a fork and removed the lids, and they helped themselves.

'I only have beer in the fridge. Can't drink any myself, but I can crack a can for you.'

'Thanks.'

He did, and they returned to the sofa which, being a two-seater, meant they sat close and friendly.

Pretending she didn't feel in the least bit awkward and had forgotten all about that uber-friendly eye in the hallway earlier, Amy said lightly, 'So how's Fossicker's Gully tonight? Celebrating?'

'More or less. Everyone's being sensible so far, but the night's young.' He paused.

'Haven't had a chance to ask about your morning in Maryborough.' She groaned. 'Didn't turn up a thing.'

Amy poured out the details and her frustration while Alex patiently finished his food and listened.

'Sorry it's been a brick wall so far. More beer?' he asked as she drained her can.

'No, thanks. Need a clear head for thinking.'

'You've come up with something.'

'It's sort of illegal.' She paused. 'You won't like it.'

Alex heaved a long sigh and growled, 'Spit it out.'

72

'Obviously I can't go around there and knock on the door, so I need to break into Stephen's place.'

Alex sat forward and laced his hands together between his knees. 'Amy — '

'Before you say anything,' she said desperately, taking the liberty of resting a hand on his nearest arm without thinking and felt his body warmth through the sleeve, 'I need to see Kelly's birth certificate. Something's not right. I get a feeling we've all been tricked about her mother's name and I'm looking for the wrong one.'

Alex sat in strained silence, shaking his head.

'It's my brother's house, so technically it's not really breaking in, is it? I mean, I'm family, right?'

'Doesn't make it legal,' he said tightly.

Corrected, Amy withdrew her hand from his arm.

'How will you get in?'

'With a key,' she boasted. 'You're not a pot-plant guy, but my trusting brother is.'

'Okay, you can get in. Where will these certificates be?'

'In the filing cabinet in Stephen's office. You know my brother. He's organised and predictable. If I'm looking for certificates, they'll be filed under C.'

'And when exactly is this *event* happening?'

'In the morning while they're at church. Service is at ten; he and Kelly will be sitting in a pew by fifteen minutes before. I'll be in the house by then and back before you can say amen.'

'All being well,' Alex clarified.

'It will. Promise. I rarely receive an invitation to the townhouse, but I know my way around the place.'

'How do you plan on getting there without being seen? It will be broad daylight and neighbours can be nosy.'

'Sunday morning streets are quiet, but you know that old access lane off Reef Road?'

Alex nodded. 'Runs right along the side of Stephen's place.'

'Exactly. I'll go down the end of this street, walk the two blocks among the trees to Reef Road, wait till it looks clear, and head down past the houses on the left into the lane.'

'With that sore shoulder, can you scale Stephen's back fence?'

'Sure.' Well, she wasn't exactly, but she needed to sound positive. 'And their back yard is entirely private from neighbours. I won't be seen.'

Another tense silence lingered between them. She wasn't game to speak. She could see Alex processing her plan and not liking it one bit. They both knew, with or without his approval, she would carry it out anyway.

'I'm afraid I've given you more than enough leeway and too much rope on this quest to hang yourself.'

In the light of the deep and genuine concern on Alex's face, Amy acknowledged the extent of his involvement in her search and turned suddenly contrite. 'I know,' she admitted softly. 'I've stretched our friendship, and I apologise for putting you in an awkward position, but this is

74

not just about me. It's about Stephen and possibly my whole family. It was attempted murder, Alex. It's serious.'

'Understood,' he replied bluntly, 'but take every care while you're out.' His glare was thunderous.

'I will. I promise.'

'Don't make promises you can't keep. This little *excursion* of yours could go belly up.'

'I hope not,' Amy countered in alarm. 'I've thought it out. I'll be fine.'

'What if you're seen and recognised?'

'I can't think like that.'

'You should.'

'I'll be super careful.'

Alex pushed himself to stand and gathered up their plastic containers. 'I'm heading out again for a couple of hours. You should try and get more sleep. You'll need it.'

'I slept all afternoon,' she protested.

Amy watched him stride across the room and knew she had pushed way beyond her boundaries with him, but there was one more favour she needed to ask. Her long list of paybacks was adding up.

'I'm guessing you keep disposable gloves in the station?' she ventured.

Alex tossed her a knowing tolerant glare.

'They would be less bulky than rubber dishwashing gloves. Just sayin'.'

'I'll grab the box on my way back later,' he said quietly.

She mouthed *thank you* as he strapped on his official gear, cap and vest again, and was gone.

With Alex back out on duty, Amy used the quiet solo time to tweak the following morning's plan in her mind. Just before midnight, she heard his vehicle return, and footsteps. Not surprising he looked beat, having rescued her just after dawn and been on duty ever since.

Amy smiled weakly. 'The Gully settled for the night?'

'The stayers are still celebrating. Benny will keep me up to speed if he sees trouble on his regular night patrols. And I've asked him to swing by Stephen's place and report any movements overnight. It's been a long one.' He kicked off his boots and disappeared.

When he returned, Amy took one long indulgent look and her heart dissolved. Changed from his uniform and showered, dark wavy hair still beaded and damp, she tried not to stare at the casual revived transformation. She had seen him in civvies plenty of times in the past six months since his return. But this close and personal, at this hour, isolated from the usual busyness of her daily working life on a newspaper, the intimacy of the late night moment intensified her emotions into overdrive.

From the lingering glance that connected their gazes, Amy just bet Alex could see the soppy adoration on her face. Hard to wipe it, really. She wondered if he felt anything for her or if this lifetime longing would ever be returned. He seemed to appreciate her as a woman. Question was, did he still regard her as Stephen's little kid

76

sister, or Amy all grown up now?

She was growing familiar with these awkward flashes of suspended time between them, but Alex, bless him, stepped in.

'So I guess you're not turning in any time soon.'

'No. I'll stay up for a bit.' Shameful to admit she had waited for his return. 'I don't mind being alone if — '

'Nah, I'll keep you company while my mind and body wind down.' He paused. 'Want a wine or a coffee?'

Amy shook her head and tucked up her legs as Alex settled beside her. She found his proximity heady but confronting. One-on-one private conversations with the idol of her fascination never happened.

'I know why I came back to town,' he drawled. 'Why did you?'

His abrupt question took her a moment to digest. Was he just being polite, or did a deeper interest lurk behind his curiosity and that disarming soft expression on his face? She lived in hope.

Amy would have preferred hearing every last detail of his own story. She rolled a response around in her mind, working out exactly how much to tell. Keep it short, she figured. At this hour and until she knew the scope of his concern, best stick to facts like a newspaper article.

'I left to study journalism in Melbourne, as you probably guessed.'

He nodded. 'Stephen kept me up to speed.'

She wasn't totally surprised to hear it. Over the years, the mates had kept in touch and would have swapped information.

'Could have gone to Bendigo but wanted to spread my wings. As part of my degree, besides the usual coursework I did a placement in a city newsroom. Discovered I loved the written word and traditional journalism. The digi age is a fast tool, but getting to know people on a deep level and hearing their stories, writing features, that sort of thing interests me more. So after nearly five years of uni and my master's, I spent another two years in the city gaining work experience in the industry.'

Amy shrugged. 'But as it happens, something was missing and I started hankering for peace and quiet and nature. A sense of place, I guess. Belonging. So when I heard our former editor, Teddy Williams, was leaving after his long stint with the *Standard* here, I applied. Thank goodness they snapped me up, because I would probably be living somewhere else in the country by now for sure. That was five years ago, but it's been so busy seems like only two.'

'Not dissatisfied or restless?'

'Hell no. I'm my own boss. We have the usual deadlines, which goes with the business, but apart from the occasional flurry day, there's no undue pressure. I love it. I leave the office and in five minutes I'm home. No long commute at the end of the working day. My car practically knows its own way back to my cabin, where I'm instantly in nature. I love to run and cook, and I'm dabbling with a bigger project. A book,' she admitted with a degree of reserve.

'Well you always have plenty to say. I can see you getting that all down on a keyboard.'

Amy chuckled. She was growing to love this lighter teasing humour, an expansion of the boyish ribbing Alex dished out in their youth.

'And I have two of the best co-workers. Michael's our main reporter and photographer. After graduating, he spent two years in the city. Been with us for two years now, but he's a steamroller. Nothing stops him getting a story. Kind of guy who would love to find a whistle blower and create headlines. He thrives on controversy. He'd probably be happy in a war zone.' She grinned. 'Can't see him hanging around much longer.' Amy sighed. 'It's going to mean another staff search. Not easy tempting people out into the country. I figure we've been lucky to have Michael this long.

'And then there's our young Georgia. She's the office junior. Did a one-year diploma to get into the industry and is part time at university in Bendigo. She's social media savvy and has really put the *Standard* out there into the world. She's physically gorgeous, yet shy, but I can see her blossoming soon, maybe into a radio studio and podcasting or even in front of a TV camera. She does all our ads and notices and classifieds, club and sports reports.'

'And what about you?'

'I scout for advertising. Keeps us solvent,' she quipped. 'Do features, edit, proof. Pull each edition together. Share the workload of the other two. Michael will love being in charge while I'm missing.' A grin tugged the corners of her mouth.

'So what does your working week look like?'

Amy glowed that his questions probed further into her life and career, suggesting that possible greater bond she craved. For some reason she needed to tell him, and equally wanted to know more about his own intervening years when they had been apart. In their childhood trio with Stephen, she had always come last.

'No day is ever the same. Phoning people and emailing. Out and about. Part of my job is just knowing what's going on. You've seen the *Standard* office. It's nothing fancy. A shop front on Main Street, a front counter, three desks and computers with a kitchen and facilities out the back. We might only have a readership of a couple thousand, and each edition might be thin on pages, but its production each week is rewarding. It's a vital part of district life. Working on a country newspaper is still busy, but at a slower pace. It's almost like community property. Residents might be bored by global news, but they like to read about their neighbours.

'You mentioned old Eddie Ryan earlier today. He usually brings in a full bowls club report every week. Stands at the counter for a chinwag. We usually offer him a chair and run to a cuppa. Since being widowed and with his family all living away, he appreciates the company. Must get lonely still living out on the farm. I imagine the bowls club is his saviour. By the way, have you heard how he's doing?'

'Yeah, swung by the medical centre before. He

80

checked out okay. Refused to stay in overnight, but Helen suspects he might need to be assessed. If he blacked out before the accident, it could be a memory or health issue.'

'He must be in his eighties. Same era as old Augie Temple.'

Both grew reflective. Amy knew she had talked about herself more than she intended. She wondered how much Alex would be willing to share and decided to find out.

'So, Sergeant Hammond, why did you leave Fossicker's Gully all those years ago, and why did you come back?'

6

Amy worried that Alex hesitated and frowned when she switched the focus to him. Surely he had been asked before? Opened up to Stephen in the past. Or maybe he really wasn't prepared to talk about it.

Eventually he said quietly, 'Needed to work off some immaturity and unhealthy anger. I felt guilty deserting my mother and leaving all my younger siblings instead of staying and standing up for them against a drunken useless father. But I needed to get out, grow up and see what else the world offered. It taught me how life could be different.

'Funny, but over time, I also grew to realise that the Gully was home, I belonged here and it needed protection.' He shrugged. 'Something called me back, and with Jim getting out of prison again, I decided to give my hometown another shot.'

Personally, Amy was glad he had made that decision, but wondered how long the Gully could hold and satisfy a man of honour and integrity like Alex Hammond.

'Maybe now I can right a few wrongs. Give something back to the town that raised and helped shape me, thanks to Stephen.' He pulled a wry grin.

'Even back then you knew you'd return?'

'Yeah, someday. But not when or for how

long.' He looked away from her across the room, his thoughts clearly distant for a time. 'So I became a nomad. Seeking work to fund my adventures. Kept in touch with Selma. Grew physically and mentally stronger. Saw how good people and good men lived. Five years ago when I decided to return, I joined up.'

'From what you've just said, I think I get why you chose the police force.'

He grinned, and the relaxed expression that spread across his face changed his whole demeanour. 'Yeah. I'd already learnt to look out for myself and watch my back, so personally I was in the right place and ready for a service career. Did a few years of general duties in stations, building career skills. You get posted as needed around the state. More transfers if you're single. If you volunteer for a position, you receive priority.'

'Is that what happened with the Gully?'

'Yep, pretty much. I'd heard whispers from Stephen that Sergeant Mitchell was retiring, so when the position came up, I applied.'

'No regrets?'

The steady gaze he levelled over her took Amy's breath away. 'Absolutely not.'

Stated with such firm conviction and an undercurrent of meaning, she smiled to herself but stayed silent. Which was easy. Listening to his deep hypnotic voice was like free therapy.

'Being a policeman is a big community responsibility and a duty as much as a job, especially out here in the country. But like you, I enjoy dealing with people across behaviour, crime, accidents, emergencies and always that endless corro. Paperwork,' he explained when Amy raised her eyebrows. 'Need to document and report everything. Attention to detail might mean a conviction or a criminal walking free. Sad to see such a rise in domestic troubles, though. Couples tend to keep a lid on it, especially the women. Shame.'

From his generous sharing of confidences, Amy began to understand the depth of his work that people took for granted.

'How's your own family?' Amy wasn't sure if it was wise to ask, but the conversation kind of swung in that direction. 'I see Selma still riding her bike around town.'

Alex shrugged, and a softness crossed his face as he spoke of his mother. 'She works too hard but she's surviving. Old man's due for release soon. Lisa's in a poor relationship and has a daughter, Gracie, as you probably know.'

Amy nodded. 'I've seen her once or twice. She's adorable.'

'Julie seems to be the only one with a sensible head on her shoulders.'

'She's a favourite in Gwennie's salon. Everyone goes there. Julie's fully qualified now.'

'Yep. Intends to buy the business when Gwen retires.'

'Hard to imagine but it could happen.'

Amy found it uplifting to talk about their shared knowledge of their hometown. At least they had that in common, even if there was always this bridge between them that held them both back from being more than Stephen's kid sister and his best mate.

'My kid brother Billy's amazing with his hands. Should do mechanics or engineering. Trying to get him to realise he can make a change and stop being a victim. He's a work in progress.'

'With an older brother like you as a role model, he'll succeed.'

He looked up and his lazy glance settled over her. Again. 'Thanks. Hope so. Knowing my background, that's a generous thing for you to say.'

'You've risen above your past. You and Stephen connected right through school and he thinks highly of you. Me, too,' she added warmly.

'I was all too aware of the differences in our families. Couldn't have been socially further apart, huh?'

Amy shrugged. 'Sure, according to the narrow-minded snobby few around here,' she clarified.

They were just three kids hanging out and having fun. Two from wealth and privilege, and the poor disadvantaged rebel and felon's son. Back then, David Randall disapproved of their association. Jim Hammond, on the other hand, didn't know or care where any of his kids were or what they did. Selma was the provider in that family and did her best to create a stable, if humble, home.

As adults now each doing their own thing with their lives having changed and moved on, it no longer mattered. Neither she nor Alex and certainly never Stephen gave their former perceived social disparity any weight or thought. They were equals. Thinking back, their friendships had always been so, and all three had made good.

Finished remembering, Amy sighed. 'I was aware of differences but it never bothered me. Dad drummed his Randall expectations into us. I just thought our father's attitude was plain mean and unchristian, considering they sat in a pew most Sundays. Stephen ignored him and defended you one hundred percent. Wouldn't hear a bad word about you. Said you were tops at sport, worked hard in class, and he considered you honest and reliable. He was your biggest fan.'

Alex shuffled in embarrassment. 'Well, we certainly clicked as mates right from the start when we were boys on the footy field. Stephen was a good sportsman, played fair, and I admired him for that. We both knew we could depend on each other and always had each other's backs. I felt awkward at first. A friendship with a Randall seemed unlikely for any son of Jim Hammond, but right from the start your brother made it clear that didn't bother him.'

'It wouldn't. He takes after Mum like that. She's the softie. Dad's old-school tough.'

He tossed her a grinning side glance. 'Often wondered why you wanted to tag along with us and not a bunch of girlfriends.'

Well, that was a loaded question that she couldn't honestly answer without blushing, so she stalled and crinkled her nose. 'Girly stuff never really appealed. I preferred tramping around the bush with you guys instead of experimenting with clothes and makeup. Probably why I never really had any close girlfriends. Even now all my classmates have pretty much all left town. A few stayed, and we acknowledge each other about town since I've been back working on the *Standard*, but only casually. What can I say? We're not really on the same page anymore.'

'Thought you'd be more social,' Alex commented.

Amy shrugged 'I guess I was during uni and my years working in the city. Not so much since I've been back home. My life's been about work and family. Plus I didn't have much spare time for the two years I was renovating the cabin.' She glanced across at Alex. 'I know it used to bug Stephen when I kept pleading, but he usually let me trail along with you two. Growing up, boys were easier company. Girls can be bitchy.'

The atmosphere in the room had grown softer, yet intense.

'Stephen often asked me if I minded.'

'Did you?'

'Course not.'

'You hardly noticed me.'

'Oh I knew you were around,' he drawled. 'You had spunk and you were cute with that swinging ponytail.'

He'd been aware of her even as a kid?

Delighted to hear it and receive even the crumb of a perceptive compliment, Amy played down the promising effect of his warm words. 'Yeah, I was just a scrawny preteen.'

'Only for a while,' he said, 'but you amused me.'

And she thought he hadn't been paying attention. On reflection, had all that boyhood teasing been flirting? Had his family background and that glowering radical image held him back?

Amy felt a stab of disappointment for him that he'd not had the courage to step forward. Being five years younger than both boys, she was only an emerging teen while he and Stephen had almost finished school. Her brother heading to university and a law degree while Alex left the country. Disappearing from her life overnight.

Amy well remembered the piercing ache of devastation when he was gone. Stephen returned home for uni breaks and the long summer holidays, but Amy believed she would never see Alex again.

As she matured, she recalled her deep crush over Alex, seeing it in the light of an embarrassing fond nostalgia. She put her feelings down to growing up and tried to forget him, but all through her high school years and university her determination was only made harder each time Stephen mentioned any contact from Alex somewhere in the world.

So he never really left her mind. Or her heart.

Even then, it was a bolt of surprise when Stephen announced his mate's return to Australia. Alex Hammond back home. Amy's first thought and only concern was whether he had brought back a girlfriend or partner or, even worse, a wife. And hated herself after all the intervening years for still feeling any interest in him.

'Glad I entertained you,' Amy said lightly.

'You seemed so young at the time. For an older teenager, and with my rocky reputation, I knew to keep my distance.'

'Old Mitchell caught you out once or twice.' Amy frowned. 'But I trusted you, Alex. Always.'

'Thanks. Good to know. I pushed authority. Defence kicking in because Mitchell always seemed to be knocking on our front door first whenever there was trouble in town. Standing there looking smug in his police uniform.'

'He was like that. Pompous.'

'Well I guess I didn't have much going for me in the character department and he was letting me know.'

'All the senior girls in high school were hooked on your wicked smile and easy charm.'

'What did you think?'

Amy grinned. 'I wasn't immune.'

Alex ducked his head then glanced up again, dark eyes shadowed, his expression serious. 'With my bad attitude and your family status around town, I didn't believe I was good enough for you, Amy. You deserved someone better.'

'Cripes, Alex.' Amy straightened, her head and heart bursting with his admission. 'We knew you hated authority, but even in your teens you had that moody raw male appeal. You must know you were a chick magnet.'

'Maybe back then.'

Amy wildly shook her head. 'Still are,' she

objected. 'Amazed there's no woman in your life.'

'I've fielded a few offers in recent months.'

Which set Amy thinking who. She would never ask and wouldn't expect Alex to tell. 'I can imagine.' She hesitated before adding, 'Alex, you must know you're the best cop the Gully's ever had. At least in our lifetime. The whole town breathed out a collective sigh of relief when old Sergeant Mitchell retired. He'd been flexing his power and taking it easy for years.' She sent out a challenge. 'You don't still believe that, do you? About not being good enough for a woman?' She generalised, avoiding making this about her.

'No. And we're talking about you specifically here.'

'Are we? Good. Because you already know Stephen and I never gave that any consideration.'

'I know. But Stephen doesn't come into *us*, does he?'

'Us?'

'*Our* friendship. You and me. We're adults now, and seems to me it's a whole different ballgame.'

'I guess so.'

Because the direction of their discussion was growing scarily personal again, her heart pounding with unvoiced promise, Amy's usual confidence deserted her and she changed topic, afraid to own these freshly developing feelings.

'I should let you turn in. My fault you've had a long day.' She uncurled her feet and rose.

Perhaps sensing the reason for her hesitation,

he said evenly, 'My bedroom is still yours.'

She wished. 'Where will you sleep?'

'I'll set up a camp mattress in my office.'

'I feel bad.'

'Don't. I've slept rough in the most unlikely places. Not a problem.'

He was so darn masterful and adaptable. The kind of guy who would sure look after his woman and be sexy as all get out doing it. Yet she knew, all the while still allowing that lucky girl to be herself. She liked that.

Alex Hammond wouldn't be attracted to Barbie dolls. He'd like his woman independent. Bit of spirit. Sense of adventure maybe. Someone accepting of his career choice and its dangers while pursuing her own.

She halted her thoughts. She could almost be thinking about someone exactly like . . . herself. Amy's heart kicked over with a thrill of possibility. And why not? They were both free and single. He seemed to like her. Could be even more than a little interested as a mature woman now and not the kid he once knew.

Might be worth watching him more closely and check out his body language. She'd been so out of it mentally since the tunnel, desperate for sleep, but that issue was sorted now and her brain crystal clear again to soak up any vibes.

He had already mentioned thinking she was once cute and amusing, but she'd never been a woman to push herself forward for romance. If a bloke was keen, then he could do the leg work. If there were sparks, naturally she would respond. Where Alex Hammond was concerned, in her own body fireworks were already fizzing and exploding. Only time would tell if he could ever feel the same.

It had been something like seventeen hours since Alex gallantly came to her rescue in the tunnel. He was and always had been her hero. Proof from his gentleness today in tending her gunshot abrasion. And, despite his objections, agreeing to put the law on hold and wait while she further investigated Kelly.

To get more information and background on her sister-in-law and hopefully evidence to support Amy's claim of an alleged attack to prove Kelly's guilt. When that happened, she would report the offence and make an official statement, inevitably leading with both Augie and Alex as reliable witnesses to charges being laid, no doubt ending with her brother's wife being sent to prison.

As yet the story and reason behind the attempted murder still remained a mystery. Amy only hoped it didn't take much longer to solve. But she was a newspaper sleuth with a curious mind who firmly believed the truth would come to light, uncovering Kelly's secret and criminal behaviour.

Briefly, once or twice today, Amy had questioned whether she should have just reported the incident. Besides thin evidence and the two women's words against each other, Amy had a burning need to know more.

Then there would be the inevitable uproar in the Randall family. Stephen's horror at his wife's reality and her own personal conflict that the truth should be reported in her own local newspaper. Not to forget the fallout around town. The gossip that would spread like a summer bushfire in tinder-dry grass.

Her own professional experience had taught her to pull back and wait. And instinct told her again that if she could identify Kelly's motive, she would have a stronger case to pursue in court.

Highly irregular of her in asking Alex to wait and give her time to privately investigate, of course. At first, his reluctance had strained their friendship; yet after tonight, she felt they were drawing not only physically but emotionally closer while she was in his flat and, in a sense, underground.

'Ames?'

Alex's familiar voice was close as she emerged from her place in deep thought. She refocused to find him standing beside her in the hallway. She didn't even remember moving across the room to get here.

'Sorry?'

A lazy smile pulled his gorgeous mouth wide. 'I lost you there for a moment.'

'Thinking about the morning and . . . stuff.' How lame did that sound?

Then he astonished her and did the unimaginable. Pressed those beautiful lips across her cheek soft and gentle. There was an abrupt awkward moment afterwards when he drew back and they both seemed to be working out exactly what the kiss had meant.

To Amy it signalled fondness. A caring mushy

side to a macho man, and her skin still tingled from the feather-light graze he had brushed across her skin.

Only Alex himself knew what it meant to him, since he had made the spontaneous move.

It was the first time ever in their whole lives of knowing each other they had shared more than an accidental touch. This one had been intimate and deliberate. The buzz it set burning inside her needed some consideration. After Amy was so tenderly kissed, her instinct had been to slide her arms around that strong safe body and snuggle against him.

And those big brown eyes belonging to Alex revealed he was more than a little stunned, too. Caught out maybe when his intention had been platonic and innocent enough. Only to have his reaction backfire into a shocked attraction.

They both held each other's gaze and teetered on the edge of wondering if he would dare to act on his instinct and kiss her again. Up to him. Amy prayed.

Her hopes fell and her pleasant surprise turned to disappointment when he stepped back and cleared his throat. 'Get more sleep for the morning. You're going to need it.'

So that was that. She sighed. 'You worry too much.'

'Possibly. I left the box of disposable gloves on the kitchen bench.'

'Thanks. Night, Alex.'

'Night.'

★ ★ ★

Amy settled in Alex's bed, stretched out flat, eyes wide open in the dark. Thinking about him. His confidences tonight, sharing his life. The deep rumble of his voice as she listened to him talk. The more-than-friendly cheek kiss. So swift and gentle it had almost never happened.

And behind all that, her subconscious intruding and dwelling on tomorrow as she itched to find a copy of Kelly's birth certificate and find out the real identity of her mother. No need to set the alarm. She usually woke with the daylight and her mission wasn't an early start. It was the sweet remembered feel of Alex's lips that sent her to sleep.

★　★　★

Alex lay on his back on the airbed in his office, hands behind his head. Well aware Amy slept right next door. In his bed. He had impulsively kissed her because those green eyes looked so vulnerable. With that silky raven hair rustling about her shoulders with any movement of her head, he tended to lose concentration when she was around.

The kid sister had sure grown up. He'd been watching her from a distance for six months and regretted staying away from his hometown so long. He missed Amy's transition from leggy teen before blooming into the full potential of the strong modern woman somehow he knew she would always become.

In the morning he would patrol by Stephen's place while she was inside. It constituted a break-and-enter even if it was family and the property known to Amy. Which, as the law in town, he was ignoring. His decision didn't sit well with him, but he was discovering fearless Amy was making him edgy and protective. Plus he was a cop. It was his duty, surely, to watch out for one of Fossicker Gully's own?

7

When Amy woke next morning, her forthcoming *excursion*, as Alex put it, immediately came to mind. She made sure she dressed before padding barefoot out to the living area. Just in case.

But as she passed his open office-cum-bedroom door, she noticed his mattress was empty and his bedding already neatly folded. A fellow early riser. A person was having trouble finding any faults here.

The rebellious bad boy, always testing limits, had changed to become a methodical and self-reliant man, his restless energy now channelled into the law and his community.

Strange to be seeing him close up in a new light. He was no longer the iconic pinup boy of town from when she was still an impressionable early teen. As a woman now, her whole body and senses reacted to this knockout god of a man who had re-entered her life and stirred sensual yet tender emotions in a totally different and very adult way.

It was barely seven, but Alex was already in the kitchen and dressed for work. Which made Amy aware how much his career dominated his life. Especially in a small country town when he was always on call.

Man, he looked gorgeous. The dark uniform colours suited him and his fit lean body perfectly filled out every inch. Amy mentally sighed.

Lingering aromas of cooked bacon and toast filtered to her nostrils.

'Morning, Sergeant,' she said wryly, yawning, impressed by his all-round abilities, no doubt acquired over the past decade, leaving Amy feeling hesitant on his home ground. Odd, because he had been so welcoming.

'Sleep okay?' She nodded. 'Cereal and toast or eggs?'

'Everything.'

Alex chuckled, pushed more bread into the toaster and set about scrambling another batch of eggs and bacon.

'If you need more clothes,' he suggested as he worked, 'while Stephen and Kelly are occupied in church I could head out to your cabin and pick up more.'

'That's thoughtful. Thanks.' She smiled and shrugged. 'You know where to find them. Another change of the same will do fine.'

After breakfast, Amy stuffed a pair of disposable gloves into her sweater pockets, dragged the beanie over her hair and headed for the door. He was too easy-going today. No advice, no cautions, so before she left, she tossed over her shoulder with a cheeky tolerant glance, 'You're going to tail me, aren't you?'

The slightest lift of his expressive eyebrows told her nothing and everything. 'Take care.'

Despite his friendly growl of warning, and although she wouldn't need it, somehow Amy found the promise of backup comforting.

While she didn't really consider she was breaking any laws, she was giving them a decent bend, fully aware that none of her efforts in solving the challenge of her sister-in-law's true background and reason for attempted murder would have been possible without Alex's compliance.

Amy had always pushed boundaries that brought on the inevitable scrapes, but readily accepted and handled any consequences. So she knew her actions challenged Alex, who had stepped sideways from his past youthful defiance to a man of redeemed character with a deep sense of honesty and ethics.

Their one single clash being her approach to Kelly's crime and decision to delay reporting the critical shooting in the tunnel on Friday night, leaving a would-be murderer loose in the community and her brother's life in danger.

For Amy to be out on the quiet Sunday morning streets of Fossicker's Gully was a welcome breather from being confined inside Alex's flat. Her injured arm was achy and stiff but bearable.

To her relief, a light fog had drifted down. She missed her runs through the bush. Her body and muscles hankered for the exercise and freedom. And she longed to be back to what she might only last week have considered her ordinary life, but instead her mission called for more hiding away a while yet.

Honestly, if this morning's efforts didn't yield results, she would spit dust.

With lots of side glances and looking back over her shoulder, Amy slunk along to the gravel road at the end of Main Street, striding across to shelter behind the thick lacy screen of peppercorns on the other side. They offered perfect cover for two blocks east to Reef Road, where she halted. She checked her phone clock. Ten minutes early. She would wait.

At almost ten, she figured she was safe to make a footpath dash along the road to the laneway access at the rear of Stephen's townhouse. A few people were on the street but too far down to be recognised. She waited, watching and listening for any nearby cars starting up, voices or doors slamming.

Nothing.

So she sprinted, breathing hard, adrenalin making her heart race as she remained alert. Only feeling out of danger once she turned into the lane and ran to the familiar paling fence running along the side of Stephen's place.

Casting a hurried glance back down the lane to the street, again her eyes and ears peeled for any neighbourhood activity, Amy scaled the fence and jumped down into the garden bushes on the other side. A dog yapped somewhere close so she froze to stillness a moment. Couldn't be inside her brother's house because Kelly hated pets.

She gave her mind and pounding heart a chance to settle, then headed for the back porch. Leafy pot plants sat green and lush either side of the door.

Amy closed her eyes, prayed, and began exploring underneath among the foliage. Nothing in the first one so she tried its mate. Nothing there either. She rummaged around both pots again. Zilch. Damn. Either the key had been moved someplace else or it wasn't here at all. She simply hadn't bothered with a plan B, believing it unnecessary. *Lesson learned, Amy.*

Aware of the minutes ticking away, she cast a frantic gaze quickly about nearby. Tried another pot plant further along, even stood on tiptoe and ran her hand above the doorframe. Still nothing.

Amy cursed. If this was a wild goose chase and she couldn't even access the house ... She squatted, heart thumping. *Think, Amy.*

In desperation, she checked the three rear windows. All locked. These days, even in country towns where once doors might have always been left unsecured, most people played safe and locked up. Amy imagined Kelly would be paranoid about that.

She stood, hands on hips, fingers tapping. Time was marching on. She needed to get inside. As her furrowed brow and frustrated gaze roamed the rear garden, she scanned for anything out of place that might suggest a hiding place for a spare house key. Of course there was also the unthinkable scenario that there was no damn key here at all.

Five long and wasted agonising minutes had ticked by. She had allowed thirty minutes in Stephen's office before the morning progressed and more people were about, giving her enough time to retreat and get back to Alex's flat, so she needed to find that key soon or retire and give up. But defeat was a word that a curious journalist never really allowed to enter their mind.

101

Amy focused and thought again. Stephen was in office management and a lawyer, so the key should be in a plausible place. Where could he have moved it?

On television, she had seen fake rocks planted in gardens with a magnet and recess beneath that held a key. She walked along the garden beds and searched for anything that seemed a likely possibility. Something unusual or misplaced, but nothing caught her attention.

She turned back toward the townhouse. Logically, the key should be hidden somewhere around that back door. Amy checked her phone again. Ten minutes behind now.

She crossed her arms, tried to relax the building tension in her body, and let her gaze freely roam. What was different or new about the house? Amy reassessed. Her eyes settled on the door knocker. Why would they have one of those on the back door? It was in the shape of a long leaf. It matched the house so didn't unduly draw the eye but blended into its position.

Amy hardly dared hope as she strode toward the house, slid on the disposable gloves from her pockets, put a hand on the door knocker and hesitated a second before she flipped it right up.

Bingo.

How damn lucky was that?

She sagged with relief, removed the key and clenched it tight in her hand. Shaking, she let herself inside and slipped the key safely back under the knocker.

She stood still a moment, listening, then crept upstairs. Stephen's office was its usual vision of order. Hardly a piece of paper on his desk, its surface gleaming. Kelly's handiwork no doubt. But she made straight for his filing cabinet, pulled out the top drawer and scrambled along the folders to C until she found *Certificates*.

She opened it on the desk, kept an eye on his wall clock — damn, half an hour eaten up already — and flipped through.

Gosh, he had received heaps of shooting awards lately. Kelly's prizes from last spring festival. The marriage and birth certificates, then, would be further down, since they seemed to be in order of date. Although she itched to rush, Amy made herself slow down and progress methodically through each document.

Halfway down, she hit pay dirt. A large crisp envelope with Marriage Certificate printed on the front. Amy's heartbeat quickened in anticipation as her gloved fingers fumbled to open the unsealed back flap. When she withdrew the certificate, her expectations were immediately dashed. Kelly Bates. Alice Bates.

Damn. This was too much. She thumped her fist on the disappointing document. But she whipped her phone from her coat pocket, tapped the camera icon and photographed it anyway.

Amy slid the certificate back into its envelope and kept working her way further down. Maybe the birth certificate? Usually optimistic, Amy grew despondent.

Suddenly the landline phone rang downstairs and on the office extension, piercing the silence. Amy jumped. Jeepers. She clutched her pounding chest. Its shrill ringing echoed through the house and eventually stopped. The answering machine clicked on and Stephen's familiar voice sounded across the quiet office but the caller didn't leave a message.

Distracted, Amy refocused and continued flicking through Stephen's certificate folder. Finally his and Kelly's birth certificates appeared toward the bottom. Pushing aside her growing fear and frustration, Amy suspected failure even before she read them.

Ever so slowly, her gaze scanned Kelly's document. Kelly Bates. Father unknown and again, clearly printed, her mother named as Alice Bates.

This couldn't be right.

According to Amy's research all day yesterday through census, voting and death records until the privacy cut-off point, the Alice Bates she sought didn't exist. The woman simply had not been found.

Kelly must have given a false name for her mother. So if she wasn't Alice Bates, who was she?

Annoyed to have wasted most of Saturday looking for a fictitious name and more time this morning on a futile search, an irritated Amy took photos, returned the file to order and replaced the folder back in the filing cabinet.

She checked her watch. Time was running out. She needed to scoot. Halfway downstairs, Amy heard a car engine outside in the driveway and the roller door rumble. The inside door giving direct access from the garage into the house lay at the foot of the stairs.

She needed to make it within seconds in order to pass, escape out the back door and scale the fence into the lane.

Spurred on by adrenalin, she leapt down the stairs two at a time, whipped left down the hall to the rear door and let herself out. She crossed the lawn, scrambled over the fence and had just dropped out of sight into the lane when she heard Kelly's voice.

'Stephen, my love, the back door was unlocked. Did you forget to check it before church?'

Amy cringed. She had raced through without pressing the inside lock button. She held her breath

'I thought so. Sorry, my love,' came his concerned reply.

'We can't be too careful, my love.'

'Of course.'

'I just want to water these pots before I go and visit my friend.'

Amy slunk down to the ground, backed up against the fence, unable to move or make any noise while she heard Kelly hosing the plants. At least it gave her heart a chance to slow down after the sprint and close call from upstairs.

Eventually the sound of running water stopped and Kelly returned indoors, because Amy heard the back door close and its lock click. All fell silent again.

Feeling safe to move, she kept crouched low until she reached the end of the fence line, then strode for the street. She cautiously peered around the houses, saw no one nearby at this end, and walked briskly for the cover of the trees again, the earlier fog having already lifted.

Main Street was another matter. Even away from the main shopping blocks further down, life had taken on more of a bustle in the past hour with a few walkers and more cars about. Amy didn't recognise anyone she knew well enough to be greeted or stopped, so she took the plunge, pulled the beanie lower, shrugged deeper into her coat and made straight for the police station.

Those last few steps felt like the longest of her life. The police vehicle was parked out front. Alex was back. She almost fell through the back door in relief.

He greeted her with a sense of urgency. 'You had me worried. I thought you would be back by now.'

'Minor hiccup.' Amy felt breathless with stress. 'The key was a doozy to find. I lost fifteen minutes before I found the wretched thing, so Kelly and Stephen arrived home just as I was leaving,' she gushed, sinking onto the sofa and dragging off her beanie. 'But after all that, I turned up bloody nothing new. Both certificates still had Kelly's mother as Alice Bates, so I'm stumped.'

Alex shuffled, seeming edgy. 'Well, your day is possibly about to become more interesting. Minutes ago as I pulled in here, I just saw Kelly drive off in her fancy car.'

Somehow Amy found the energy to thrust herself to stand again. 'What! Where?'

'Definitely heading toward the highway. Probably Maryborough. Hate to say it, but you should follow. Look a bit obvious if I tailed her in a police car. We don't want to make her suspicious. I kept an eye on her movements yesterday but she stayed home.'

He had? This guy was going above and beyond. Amy frowned. 'I heard Kelly say to Stephen she was visiting a friend.'

'It's a risk using Charlie's little car again, but worth checking out. You up to it?'

Amy's response was to carefully stretch her sore shoulder, heave a sigh of resignation together with a wry grin, and tuck up her long hair under the beanie again.

'Kelly has a head start, but keep your distance and good luck.'

'Thanks. I think.'

Oh my God, Amy thought as she slid behind the wheel and fired up Charlie's car again, hoping she wouldn't be recognised. After sitting around all day yesterday, Sunday had suddenly turned up full throttle. But she didn't care, because right now Kelly was her only concern and she was speeding away from Fossicker's Gully. Amy planted her foot, backed out and followed.

Alex was right. Kelly's vehicle retraced the same drive back to Maryborough that Amy had done yesterday. To visit who and for what purpose other than merely social on a Sunday afternoon, she had no idea, but her intuition kicked in. She had a good feeling about this. Her hopes and mood rose, heeding Alex's wise words to keep a safe distance from Kelly's familiar car ahead.

Near Maryborough, Amy needed to edge closer, staying a few cars behind in city traffic to keep a tail on Kelly, but her quarry turned left before the main part of town into what seemed to be a residential complex of some kind.

Amy watched from a distance and waited until Kelly parked her car and disappeared inside the building. Then she cautiously drove in and parked away from Kelly's vehicle while still being able to keep a line of sight to the front door when she reappeared.

From a sign near the main entrance with sliding glass doors, she learned the stunning and modern two-storey structure was an aged care facility with immaculate landscaped gardens. Amy certainly couldn't follow for fear of meeting Kelly, so she settled down to wait and wonder who was inside that her sister-in-law was visiting. She had said a friend. Who must have enough money to afford retirement in such classy accommodation.

Over an hour later, as Amy was just contemplating that she could really go for a coffee right now, Kelly reappeared, jumped in her car and drove away. She was torn between following or going inside. Curiosity to learn more about Kelly's *friend* won out. It was unlikely Amy would be recognised here and could lead to discovering more of her sister-in-law's real family background. So she was prepared to take the risk.

Amy locked her vehicle, crossed the car park and entered the building. At the reception desk she greeted the attendant with a pretence of some surprise.

'Was that Kelly Randall I just saw leaving? Who was she visiting today?' she said with chatty brightness.

'Her mother has just moved in.'

Amy stilled in shock. This was news. Kelly's mother was supposed to be dead. 'Oh, I didn't realise.' She pretended to be thinking. 'Her mother is Alice, isn't it?'

The receptionist shook her head. 'No, Helen.'

'Oh, of course,' Amy quickly mocked herself, but in her mind silently punched the air with excitement. Finally. The breakthrough she needed. Her mother's real name, and she was still alive. Kelly had always told the Randall family her single mother had died and she never knew her father.

'I wouldn't have thought *Helen*,' she announced carefully, 'was old enough to be in aged care,' Amy probed.

'Oh, she's not, really, but Mrs. Simpson has a medical condition with mobility issues and is one of our newest occupants of our new south wing suites.'

Mrs? Living here under a married name, no less! Amy was so dazed at this disclosure she could only stumble out the simple platitude, 'I'm so sorry to hear that.'

'Yes, it's such a pity. She had a hard life when young, but apparently she rose later on to become a private secretary to some very important people, including the CEO of that big transport company over in Fossicker's Gully.'

Amy stiffened in shock. Surely not. 'Um . . . I

guess that would be Randall Transport?' she ventured.

'That's the one!' the attendant smiled.

It took a moment for Amy to process this bombshell. Kelly's mother had worked for her father? *This* was the connection. She was getting close, but she needed to know more.

Amy reeled not only at this new and stunning revelation but that this now tied Kelly's mother to her father, their whole family and the Randall Transport business. This mystery was becoming intriguing and close to home. Kelly's mother had worked for them and now her daughter had married the boss's son! This whole scenario was looking highly incredible and suspicious. She began to imagine wildly possible scenarios, none of them reassuring.

Trying not to show her surprise, Amy casually asked, 'This looks to be an excellent facility.'

'Thank you. We pride ourselves on making this just like home for all our residents.'

'Is it only people who live nearby that come to live here?'

'Mostly. Some may come from outlying districts or further away if they want to live near family.'

'Actually, that's the reason I called in today. Could I possibly have a look around? An aunt of mine may need care soon. Perhaps I could start with the south wing?'

'Of course. You just need to sign in on the visitor's book.' The receptionist indicated a nearby side table. 'One of our staff can give you a guided tour.'

'Oh that won't be necessary,' Amy said quickly. 'I'm more than happy just to have a wander, if that's all right?'

'Of course. You understand we appreciate that you respect our residents' privacy and not enter their rooms, but you're free to wander all the public spaces. If you have any questions, just stop by the office before you leave. We're more than happy to help.'

'Thank you so much,' Amy gushed as she signed a false name. This was too easy. And growing confusing. As she strolled the wide carpeted hallways, Amy checked names on all suite doors until she found confirmation of Kelly's mother's name. Mrs. Helen Simpson.

Amy glanced up and down the hallway, her cheeky journalistic inclination rising to the fore. No one was about, and since the door was already ajar, she gently pushed it wider to peer inside. A woman, neatly dressed in lovely clothes with grey wavy hair falling softly about her pale face, dozed in a recliner by the window. She looked so frail and harmless, Amy wondered how she figured in all this upheaval.

Amy sent out a prayer of forgiveness for the intrusion for anyone who might be listening and snapped a photo of the woman on her phone. Back in the hallway, she continued wandering for another ten minutes so the receptionist wouldn't be suspicious that she hadn't stayed long.

Passing back through the entrance and signing out, Amy was offered brochures and booklets of information which she was obligated to accept before hurriedly leaving.

Headed toward Fossicker's Gully again, Amy reflected on her sister-in-law, so far guilty of lies, deception and attempted murder, covering up her family association to the Randalls, clearly wanting to remain anonymous with the intention of some kind of misguided retribution. What a switch from the cunning hostile person she hid behind to her public facade of the sweet compliant wife.

But why?

What had their family done to deserve such criminal vengeance? After her father and Stephen's roles as owners in the business, being a PA to management was the highest and most respected clerical position in the company. Kelly's mother would have been paid a generous salary. Amy knew because all four immediate family members as shareholders held an annual business meeting at which they were kept fully informed of all accounting revenue and any future plans or developments.

But despite marriage to Stephen and on their father's orders, Kelly had never been included in these meetings. Could this be her grievance?

Amy thought not, since Kelly's attempt to murder her suggested something much greater at play here. Another far more deep-seated reason behind her sister-in-law's need for reprisal.

Bubbling with excitement, Amy knew she was on the verge of solving the mystery.

8

With so many thoughts and the consequences of new information racing through her head, halfway home Amy was forced to pull over into a roadside picnic stop and reflect on today's developments. She sat for a while in stunned contemplation.

After the disillusionment of finding nothing earlier, this latest disclosure was a windfall.

The first person Amy instinctively wanted to call was Alex, but she reined in that impulse because the situation was becoming too close to home and real.

Since Kelly's intent now seemed to be a direct assault on the Randall family — for whatever reason, never enough, Amy considered, to justify such grave actions and deceit — the degree of danger it meant for Stephen living in the same house had just escalated.

It was now imperative that Amy phone her brother. She knew this meant taking yet another risk, but his life was at stake here. No time for hesitation and second chances. It was urgent she confirm exactly when and for how long Helen Simpson worked for Randall Transport to try and find out the why behind Kelly's vendetta. Clearly the answer lay with her mother.

Amy figured her mobile was probably safe to call Stephen, but being a Sunday and with Kelly due home or already back there now and in the house, she would need to use a landline. If she used her own phone, her name and number would show up. If Kelly answered, it would be a disaster. But if Amy used a public phone, her location was traceable but not her identity. So she Googled a public phone locater to discover there was usually one in most small country towns and detoured to the nearest village to make the call.

To her immense relief, standing in a phone box on the deserted main street, Stephen answered. Amy realised that, apart from Alex, he was the only other person she had spoken to for days. It was wonderful to hear his voice and know he was safe.

'Hey, sis,' he said with pleasure. 'Haven't heard from you in a while.'

'You know I'm away on assignment at the moment. And what I need to ask you is for a rather serious story I'm researching, okay? Bit of a local expose, so please don't tell anyone you've spoken to me. At all,' she said lightly, laughing. 'Sorry, bro, but that means Dad and also Kelly.' Stephen remained silent so she added, 'Need to keep a lid on it for now. Please,' she pleaded again.

'Okay, if you say so. Why all the mystery?'

'Sorry. Need to protect my source.'

Although she trusted Stephen with her life, Amy knew she was taking a risk even contacting him with their enemy living under his roof, but she had to know. The truth, whatever it turned out to be, appeared to lie so close to home within the family it was becoming both intriguing and frightening.

'It could jeopardise the impact of my article if there are leaks before it's actually published.' She squeezed her eyes shut for a moment, hating to lie to him. 'I need to know about a past employee of our company. Helen Alice Simpson.'

There was a moment of silence before Stephen responded. 'Name doesn't ring a bell. It really would be so much quicker to ask Dad,' he pointed out.

Amy's heart almost leapt out of her chest in panic. 'Oh no. Please don't. The privacy thing, remember?'

'Sure. Sounds important.'

Her brother's reassurance gave Amy a moment to take a deep breath before she continued. 'Like I said, this promises to be a rather sensitive article I'm writing and I need to keep it strictly to a need-to-know basis. I don't know the exact date of Helen Simpson's employment, but possibly when we were young, because neither of us remember her, do we?'

'No.' He paused, then asked, 'This won't implicate the business in any way?'

Amy heard the anxiety in his voice. How could she truthfully sidestep that question? For now, for his sake, she simply injected amusement into her tone and said, 'The company's safe.'

But not their family. Knowing Kelly hated Stephen working on Sundays, Amy cringed as she probed, 'Are old employment records accessible from your home computer?'

He had the grace to chuckle. He knew her too well. Her drive to gather facts for a story. 'Kelly's out visiting but she should be home soon. Then we're going for a drive and booked for dinner at the B&B restaurant.'

'Emma's place? Oh that should be nice.' Amy tried to sound happy. He was letting her know it would probably be tomorrow before Helen Simpson's information came to light. 'Well, get to it when you can. I'll appreciate it.'

'First thing in the morning.'

Not soon enough, because she felt a need for haste and a deep sense of pressure about this issue, but she said, 'Thanks. I understand. And can you email the results to Alex? He's kind of helping me with this project.'

'Sure.' He paused. 'You two seem to be in touch a lot recently. Something I should know about?' he probed with a hint of mischief in his voice.

'No,' Amy laughed, only wishing it was true.

How could they be so light-hearted when she ached to warn him about the danger to his life? When everything they considered normal was about to all change and shatter?

'Remember, not a word of my call to anyone, okay?' She felt bad for asking, but Stephen would keep his word.

'Of course. I guess we'll all know soon enough, huh?' he said lightly.

It took Amy all her courage to hang up and not blurt out the awful looming truth.

★ ★ ★

116

Amy headed her little borrowed car back toward Fossicker's Gully. To find Alex not yet home. Deprived of the thrill just yet of sharing today's awesome news about Kelly's mother, Amy pushed aside her eagerness.

Not unusual for Alex to work beyond his daily set number of hours. With his sense of duty, it often meant he was out patrolling the streets, in his office doing corro or responding to calls far longer than required. The officers in charge of one-man police stations in small country towns were leaders and role models, becoming a part of the community. Alex even more so, having been born here.

Inside his flat, Amy saw Alex had neatly placed her change of clothes on her bed. His bed. So she quickly showered, washed her hair and pulled on the fresh jeans and sweater. Then, because he had been so professionally lenient and supportive this weekend, Amy raided his fridge and freezer, finding enough ingredients for a stir fry and rice, poured herself a glass of wine and prepared dinner.

She itched to open Alex's laptop and see if Stephen had emailed yet with news of Helen Simpson's employment but knew it was way too soon. He would probably be heading out to dinner with his sweet, dangerous, two-faced . . .

Amy wanted to squeeze her sister-in-law's neck. Right now. Swoop in and drag Stephen far away from her phony clutches.

So far out of necessity since Friday night, Amy had kept plodding on, holding her composure. Yes, she had abrasions and bruises, had suffered the icy cold and dark of a tunnel for one long night, but she was alive. She had survived.

Sadly, knowing what she did now, that Helen Simpson was alive if ageing and unwell, and Kelly's deliberate secretive subterfuge to conceal the fact and infiltrate the Randall family, the level of Stephen's vulnerability to danger grew alarmingly with every second that passed. Amy grew terrified for his safety.

Based on the scale of what Kelly had done, Amy felt no guilt about breaking into the townhouse this morning. Her crime was minimal compared to her sister-in-law's scheming. Viewed overall, the deception and criminal intent were bad enough, but their exposure, which was growing closer and inevitable, was going to mean destroying the heart and soul of the intelligent warm-hearted brother she held so dear.

In Amy's mind, whatever punishment ensued could never compensate for the fact that as the result of such an abhorrent betrayal, Stephen's life was about to be ruined by the woman he so deeply and genuinely loved.

Maybe it was the wine causing her sadness, or maybe it was the onions she was slicing, but Amy felt tears fill her eyes and roll down her cheeks. She let them flow and made no attempt to brush them away, sniffing and weeping, finally giving freedom to the tension of recent days.

Caught up in the depths of her emotional release, of course she didn't hear Alex return.

'Amy?'

He was at her side like the strong, warm,

beautiful human being he had always been. Turning, she gave him a weak smile and a helpless shrug before he gathered her up into the comfort of his arms. He removed his police cap, but his equipment belt dug into her side.

Amy allowed herself to just be held. Firmly. For a long time. Alex didn't utter a word. Just waited quietly until he sensed she was over the worst.

'Bad news?' he murmured.

Amy eased herself away from his warm body and shook her head. He looked so stunning in that uniform. Alex produced tissues, so she wiped her face and blew her nose.

'It's exactly the opposite. Great news. A breakthrough. But now I'm even more worried about Stephen.'

Words of explanation about Kelly's visit, her mother, and the name confusion tumbled from Amy's mouth in an unstoppable torrent.

A look of disbelief spread across Alex's face when she related the events that had transpired in Maryborough and the new facts brought to light.

'I've seen plenty of mean behaviour in my time with the force, but your sister-in-law is up there with the lowest.'

Amy, too, felt sick at the depth of Kelly's lying to access/penetrate the Randall family. What hurt her the most was knowing that Stephen's exploitation was at its core. And all by such a deceptively innocent person who clearly festered hatred in her heart.

'Phoning Stephen was a risk,' Alex continued,

'but he would never break a promise.'

'I know. I don't suppose you could check your laptop?'

'Ames, it's too soon,' he said softly, shaking his head and running the back of his hand along her cheek. 'Let me change, then I'll help you with dinner.'

Somehow they managed making dinner together with a humming electric attraction zapping between them. That it should be the man of her childhood dreams returning her lifelong crush with that fiercely protective hug and touch of his skin on hers exploding their friendship into the potential for so much more, was beyond Amy's wildest cherished desires.

She had hidden this enduring fascination since forever. Now, with a mutual magnetism finally making the connection, Alex was responding with a real and powerful awareness of his own in return. She felt it from his gaze that quietly drifted over her, lingering, all through dinner.

He cleared away their meal and stacked the dishwasher. As a distraction against the building sexual frustration that stretched between them, that thrilling awareness of a new romance, Amy asked Alex if she could use his laptop.

He put on a load of washing. Cute to see such an irresistible big guy doing the daily stuff. Independent from travelling and living on his own for years, no doubt. Then he claimed the need to catch up on paperwork next door in the station.

'See you later,' he murmured and disappeared.

Probably wise. Distance was good. Although

he was hardly far away. It seemed both of them were not so much denying as avoiding the developing pull of attraction. Amy wondered when the frustration would find release, but hoped it was soon and that Alex took the lead. She had long been aware of her feelings for him but needed the open acknowledgement of this new awareness to come from him.

With Alex safely next door, at least for now, Amy did her background research all over again, this time with the correct name for Kelly's mother. To find she had lived in the region most of her life, certainly in adulthood, but never married. Instead it appeared she just falsely added the title Mrs. in any records as it suited where necessary.

As far as Amy could find, the woman never owned property, leaving her puzzled where Helen Simpson obtained the money to fund her residency in the aged care home.

A suspicion came to mind as Amy wondered how Kelly might have persuaded Stephen to advance such a large amount. Which he would never have done without a strong reason. Kelly could hardly have revealed that her mother was still very much alive, for that would have blown the whole ruse to their marriage. Unless Stephen was unaware of it and his wife had secretly acquired it somehow. But how?

Then Amy brainstormed how on earth Helen Alice Simpson was connected or derived from Alice Bates, if at all, or whether the name was merely created for convenience.

Tracing back a generation in old online

records, Amy found a birth for Helen Alice Simpson, but with so many inconsistencies, the closest she could work out was that the woman had also been born to a single mother, father's name not recorded, so probably an illegitimate birth.

So Helen Alice Simpson was probably born Helen Alice Bates to an Edith Bates for whom Amy could not find a marriage. Perhaps later on, Kelly and her mother had simply used the Bates surname when it suited them. Talk about a tangled web.

The possible dates matched up, but it seemed the Bates/Simpson women were all prone to a degree of flexibility with the truth. Which mother had passed to daughter, with granddaughter Kelly inheriting the family practice of scheming.

Whether or not the Randalls ever unravelled the Bates family tree or indeed wanted to, would be a matter mainly for Stephen and possibly their parents.

Their mother Cora would be devastated when Kelly's behaviour was exposed, for she and her daughter-in-law had formed a ladylike, if reserved, bond of sorts in their community and charity work together. Cora had readily taken Kelly under her wing, introducing her into the limited influential circles of Fossicker's Gully. Because of Kelly, Amy preferred to volunteer and support independently of family. She knew this stance was a disappointment to her mother, who accepted their differences.

And goodness knew how their father, David, would react. With his money and power, which he never hesitated to use, his first outburst was often to take an adversary to court. But not in this case. Kelly was family. Fiercely proud, her betrayal of the Randall name and reputation would cut him deep.

When this story broke, Amy was only beginning to process the breadth of the vast rippling effect that would inevitably spread across the local community and beyond.

When Alex quietly returned from the police station to the flat later, he brought Amy another glass of wine and sat disturbingly close on the compact sofa, looking over her shoulder. She could barely focus anymore. Was he moving in on her? The pull to close the laptop and turn aside to ravish him was unbearably strong. Like an ache.

'You should take a break,' he murmured somewhere near her ear, for she felt the whisper of his warm breath on her neck.

Amy closed her eyes with pleasure, sipped her wine, forgot her work and leaned back against his shoulder. 'Can I ask you something?'

'Sure.'

He kissed the valley in the dip of her neck and she gasped. This was knee weakening seductive stuff and he was a master. She blocked out thoughts of other women in the past. This was now and only them.

'You might be offended.'

'I have a tough hide.'

She took a deep breath. 'We've known each other forever, right? I'm your best mate's little sister.'

123

'I know where you're heading.'

'Is this for real?' she whispered.

She not only wanted but needed the truth, and knew she would get it from this man. They seemed to be on the same page, but she had to know where she stood before she let go. This new attraction was too precious to jeopardise.

'Damn straight.'

'Not just because we've been thrown together for a few days?'

He let out a soft sexy chuckle. 'Uh-uh.'

He couldn't talk properly because his mouth was busy. On her. In all the right places. Every time his hot lips pressed over her skin, she practically dissolved. Alex slid the wine glass from her hand and set it aside on the low table.

Then got down to business. A big warm hand found its way into her hair, cupping her head. His mouth trailed across her cheek, teased her bottom lip, and there was really nothing left for Amy to do but surrender.

He kissed her long and slow and easy, just like the man himself, as though their lips were made for each other. Needing the contact to survive. Wow, if this was a sample of his kisses, she would pass out when they made love.

Amy almost cried with joy. She had waited so long, never believing that kismet was even possible or would ever happen with this guy.

The taste and touch of him brought her to life. She let her fingers thread through his hair and linger, as his free hand found its way beneath her sweater, exploring her warm bare skin.

For Amy, this new loving felt like it was the most natural thing in the world and they already knew each other intimately. Maybe in another life? They just *fit*.

They were so involved with one another it took a moment to register a background noise. A phone. Amy suffered a pang of loss when Alex ended their kiss and drew apart with a groan.

'Damn.'

He reached for his cordless landline, rose and paced the flat while answering the official call.

'Debbie, slow down and tell me exactly what happened. Are you hurt? Is he still there? Okay, stay put and stay calm. I'll be out there in five minutes.' Alex hung up and tossed Amy a wry glance. 'Sorry. To be continued.'

'Absolutely,' she murmured.

Amy was disappointed that they would never know how the evening might have ended, but also loved the promise of an encore. If they weren't interrupted again, who knew where it could lead? Her mind went crazy with possibilities and she sipped her glass of neglected wine for comfort.

Within minutes, Alex was changed into his uniform again. He leaned over Amy, still snuggled and lonely on the sofa, stealing a lush parting kiss.

'It's a domestic. Don't wait up.'

The mood and moment were broken for now, but not the longing. Who knew when he would be back?

Later in bed, a niggling guilt hit Amy's thoughts that she could be on the verge of such happiness when Stephen was about to meet only heart-break.

Amy considered waiting up for Alex, but after the late night call decided he would be weary and deserved rest. They would catch up in the morning. And Stephen, who was always in the company office by eight, should have looked up the old employee records on Helen Simpson and emailed the results. Feeling a deep sense of frustration on both counts, Amy knew it would be a long night.

Regardless, she slept well and soundly, only stirring and vaguely aware when Alex came in and kissed her, leaving her smiling as she drifted back to sleep.

9

Amy woke and stretched luxuriously in the early morning light. Eager to see Alex again and check his laptop in case Stephen had emailed, she trotted out to the lounge to find it empty. The smell of a cooked breakfast and dirty dishes already in the sink told her he was up and already gone.

Her disappointment changed to ridiculous pleasure when he returned soon after and they greeted each other with silly smiles.

'Morning, angel,' Alex murmured, sliding an arm around her waist while they kissed.

'I thought you had already left.'

'Miss me?'

'I might have,' she teased, then grew serious. 'How did the troubled situation play out after your phone call last night?'

Everyone knew domestic violence was increasingly common in these times of busy lives, when strained relationships and divorces placed even greater pressures on divided families.

Alex sighed. 'Lots of talking and an uneasy standoff. The parents and their three kids live on a small farm just out of town. They're doing it tough. There are a few couples in the area that I know about and need to monitor. I keep in contact, drop in on them from time to time and see how they're doing. Often they're just victims of circumstances. The drought, a lost job, then tension erupts over the smallest thing.'

'Does that include your sister?'

'Sure does. Mick's hot-headed, usually with drink. I worry for Lisa and little Gracie.' His expression softened at the mention of his niece. Yet again, Amy witnessed the depth of his caring and dedication in the community.

'I guess you've already eaten, otherwise I would return the favour and do a cooked breakfast.'

'Actually I haven't. The husband came back to town with me last night and slept in the station cell. Unlocked. Just gave him time to think, pull back from family. We talked till late. Being a farmer, he's an early riser, so I just took in breakfast to him. He'll head back out to the farm now. Seems to be in a more settled place this morning.

'He promised to start attending our blokes' group counselling sessions. It's an idea I had so we're trialling it in the community with medical professional volunteers one night a week.'

'I heard about that. You started it?'

Alex nodded. 'See a lot of need for it in my work. If it only helps one man rethink and improve his life and attitude, it's worth it.'

'For sure.'

'The sessions at least give them the skills to try. I suggested it to Mick once when he was sober. I figured he might be more receptive, but he still blew my head off. He's not open to the idea and I doubt he ever will be. I've warned Lisa, but stuff can flare up just like that.' He snapped his fingers. 'Can't always predict it. Like striking a match.'

Amy wanted to smooth the furrows across his brow when he spoke of his family and violence. He seemed under pressure from all sides at the moment with Jim due out soon, Buddy apparently playing around the fringes of crime, and young Billy vulnerable and easily influenced. It seemed Lisa was in an undesirable partnership. And the backbone of them all, his mother Selma, working her butt off to keep them all together and responsible for putting food on the table.

Alex was fully loaded with family concerns. Unaware of it until recent days, Amy had unknowingly placed even more responsibility on his shoulders by seeking his desperately needed help for her own dilemma. Like many others with both police and personal troubles, Alex Hammond, besides his official position and role in town, was also often the first person to whom local people turned.

'Don't worry about me for breakfast,' Alex murmured. 'I'll just do cereal and toast.' As he poured his favourite flakes into a bowl and sliced fruit on top, he didn't look at her but added in amusement, 'Can feel you're wired. Go check the laptop.'

'Thanks.'

Amy scooted over to it, excited, even though if Helen Simpson *had* worked for Randall Transport, it would only be confirming what she had already been told and therefore nothing new. Then the challenge would lie in uncovering the explanation for Kelly's extreme aggression toward her and the ongoing threat she posed to other members of the Randall family. Particularly Stephen.

Even this early, her brother had already sent the promised email with information about Helen Alice Simpson. Amy quickly scanned it. As she anticipated, from company records, the woman had been employed for five years in the 1990s as Personal Assistant to their father, David.

'There's an interesting note here,' Amy related. 'Stephen says her termination of employment was listed as *dismissal*.' She glanced across at Alex. 'So I have the proof I need, but it still leaves me in the dark about whatever happened back then. Judging by her recent attack on me, it was big and has left a lasting impression.' Amy frowned. 'I need to know more about Helen Simpson. I know the ideal person to ask, but as usual — ' She shrugged. ' — it means taking another risk of exposure.'

'Ames,' Alex chuckled, 'when did you ever do things the easy way?'

Was she *that* headstrong? Amy pressed on. 'It's no coincidence Helen Simpson worked for Randall Transport and now her daughter has married into the family.' Alex nodded, listening intently, looking adorable. Trying to ignore the attraction and focus, she continued, 'It's clear the cause behind her mother's sacking has probably festered over the years and resulted in Kelly's deliberate arrival into our family. The two issues are connected. I just have to find out how.'

'Be careful, Amy,' Alex warned, his expression of concern visible both in words and his wrinkled forehead, making him look vulnerable.

Man, when this was all over, did she have plans for Fossicker's Gully's local cop.

'Kelly is clearly obsessed, possibly even mentally unstable,' Alex went on. 'She's already tried to kill you once for some kind of revenge. Given the chance, if she discovers you're alive, she'll be embarrassed and angry to think she failed and you fooled her. She'll be even more determined and won't hesitate to try again.'

'But revenge for what?' Amy groaned with frustration. 'In the tunnel she said I *was the first*. So it follows that Stephen's life must be in danger, too. Living in the house with Kelly, she would have the opportunity at any time to harm him.'

Which only deepened the annoying mystery running through Amy's mind why Stephen's wife was intent on eliminating sister and brother.

As Amy paced and brainstormed possible circumstances out loud and in her head, her bigger concern was needing to get Stephen away from Kelly to keep him safe before the woman had a chance to do something nasty.

'Alex, it's been three days. There's no more time to waste. Stephen must be told Kelly's a would-be murderer, and I'm the one who has to do it.' She gasped with dread and a hand went to her mouth. 'It's going to destroy him. He adores his wife, but in order for him to even start believing me, I need to get more definite evidence first to back me up and convince him it's the truth.' Amy sent an understanding gaze toward Alex. 'The only person I can talk to for

131

more background information who is a family member and old enough to help is Mum.'

Which either meant setting up a meeting someplace private or heading out to the Randall homestead property Windarrah on the western edge of town.

With canny insight, Alex read her thoughts. 'I'm not letting you drive out in Charlie's car. At night, maybe. But since you've been noticed by one of his mates, not in broad daylight.'

Here goes. 'Hide me under the blanket again?'

'Now?' he asked, his stance accepting, his tone tolerant. Amy silently thanked the Being that placed Alex Hammond into her life and nodded. 'Okay. I need to open up the station soon so phone Cora now. If she's home alone, I'll drive you out.' He turned aside in thought. 'I guess if anyone asks why I went out there I can say I'm just warning landholders about a few recent farm thefts.'

Amy understood. Locals could be nosy, and they were heading to the pointy end of their search. They needed to take extra care now.

She made the call. 'She's home. Dad's at the office already, then has a meeting in Bendigo. He'll be gone all day.'

'Okay, let's do this.' Alex headed for the door. 'I'll bring the cruiser around back.'

Before he left, Amy stepped forward and caught his arm. 'Alex, thanks. I don't know how I can ever repay you for all this.'

As serious as their investigation issue had become, Alex's dark eyes twinkled and his gaze travelled over her with interested amusement.

'Let's get this business sorted, then I believe I have a few ideas in mind about calling in your debt.'

Amy let a grin escape while her brows rose and her eyes doubled in surprise. 'I look forward to finding out what you have in mind.'

'You and me both,' he drawled and disappeared.

While Alex brought the car around, Amy's heartbeat raced at his promise. Her lifetime worship was fast becoming so much more. Her respect and yearning for Alex Hammond was now an undeniable reality because the attraction was mutual. She would always be thankful that Kelly's aim was poor and her bullets almost missed, causing minimal damage. Allowing her the chance blessing of this new hope and potential forever love in her life.

Alex and Amy repeated the routine of that other fateful drive from the old goldmine tunnel last Saturday, only this time they drove west, turning off the main road along the gravelled tree-lined driveway leading to the grand sandstone house where Amy grew up.

When Alex whipped off the blanket and she sat up, it was to see he had pulled up around the back. As she stepped from the car, her mother greeted them at the door.

Eyeing the police vehicle, she said lightly, 'Looks official. Alex, lovely to see you.'

He nodded. 'Cora.'

She glanced between them. 'Amy sounded mysterious on the phone. Come in and tell me what this is all about.'

'I can't stay, Cora.' To Amy he said, 'Let me know when you're done.'

She nodded. 'Thanks.'

Gently taking her mother's arm, she led her indoors as Alex drove away.

In the huge country kitchen, the Aga cooker took centre stage, a kettle singing on the hob. It had always been the heart of their home. Although expensive to buy and operate, Amy aspired to a small one in deep red for her cabin kitchen. Backed up against it, Amy watched Cora bustle with tea cups and saucers, a batch of freshly baked muffins smelling spicy and still temptingly warm piled on a plate, and wondered how to begin.

'Mum, my visit needs to be kept strictly secret.'

Cora looked up with raised eyebrows. 'Oh? Another one of your research articles? Tell me more.'

Amy surveyed her tall, slim mother with respect and love. Still young in her fifties in attitude and style, always so well-presented.

She caught her daughter's gaze and said easily, 'You're on edge, dear. Sit down and talk.'

'Tea will be lovely,' she said, taking a seat at the small round breakfast table in a bay window overlooking their evergreen bush garden and surrounding paddocks beyond, 'but after you hear what I have to say, you may need something stronger.'

Patient as always, Cora joined her daughter, sipped her tea, and waited.

'Might be best if you just listen till I'm

134

finished. Hear the whole story, let it sink in.'

'As you wish,' Cora said graciously.

Slowly, Amy started when she left work last Friday, meeting Kelly as arranged at the cabin, the shock of a pointed gun, the tunnel nightmare and Augie's rescue.

Her alarm was raw enough as Amy spoke, but at the mention of Augie's name, although she remained silent, Cora's previous reactions of horror and gasps of distress became sharp, piercing attention. She shuffled in her seat, a stunned expression crossing her white face. Amy presumed because of the good luck that he found her.

She continued talking, relating it all as if her emotions were on automatic. Alex being her early morning salvation in the tunnel, his backup and cooperation in every way ever since, his generosity in hiding her in his flat.

Amy couldn't break down or crumble in her narration or in the face of her mother's teary heartsick gaze, or she would never finish. She had to get out this awful burden she had carried to this quiet family matriarch who had unselfishly embraced her husband and children, their large family business and significant work in the Fossicker's Gully community as her whole life.

That her mother had done it alongside Kelly these past three years must cut deep.

But Cora needed to know and be prepared for the inevitable landslide to come soon when the appalling truth would be revealed to the locals and beyond. The media would feast for a few

135

days, and they would all need to withstand the onslaught together.

When Amy finally touched on the fact that Kelly's mother was still alive, her identity and the revelation of working for Randall Transport, Cora's chilling gasp of disgust told her daughter she had figured out the possible connection and upshot of it all.

'Kelly!' Cora shook her head, absorbed in stunned silence for the moment. 'Amy, dear, if I'd heard all this from anyone else, I would never believe it. Are you all right?'

'I'm fine. My shoulder's stiff and tender still but I'm okay.'

'What on earth was that girl thinking? This is a nightmare just hearing about it. I can't imagine how it's affecting you actually living through it.'

Amy produced the photo of Helen Simpson she had taken on her phone Sunday afternoon. 'She will be much older, of course, but do you recognise her as the woman who worked for Dad years ago?'

'Yes, that's definitely her. Helen was always quite lovely and she has aged gracefully. A pity she's so unwell at her age.'

Cora was always so generous in her compliments, especially of other women, often closely involved with her husband through the business and community. Amy had always wondered about that.

'Do you know why Helen was dismissed?'

Cora's previously easy mood turned to discomfort, 'I do recall she left suddenly and David mentioning the fact. There's always gossip,' she said quietly, holding Amy's gaze. 'Staff come and go.'

Nothing ventured. Amy took a deep breath. 'Was it because of Dad?' A tense silence hung in the air. 'An affair?' she probed softly. The word had never been mentioned before, but since the family was confronting its dirty linen . . . 'Could Helen Simpson have been pregnant?'

'Well, David would hardly admit it, would he? I made a decision long ago never to ask about any gossip.'

So there she had it. Her mother suspected her father of being unfaithful. Amy reached out and covered her hand with her own. Their tea was cold, the delicious muffins untouched.

'If Kelly is his daughter — ' Amy whispered.

'Oh, surely not.' Cora blanched. 'That would be seriously weird.'

'It would mean Kelly is — '

'Don't even say it.' Cora rushed on, 'Whatever the situation, Stephen is in danger, correct?' she clarified.

'Deeply.' They exchanged a glance of mutual alarm. 'Now that you've given me more details about Helen Simpson, I can go to Stephen. He has to be warned. And fast.'

Amy was already on her phone texting Alex that she was ready.

'I'm sorry I don't have a driving licence, dear,' her mother apologised. 'Foolish of me to never learn. I could have taken you back to town.'

'No drama.' Amy brushed off her concern with a smile. 'Alex won't mind.'

Cora's vacant expression of distraction as she

137

stared out the window, probably not seeing the lovely rural view, made Amy suspect this whole sorry business was about to fracture more than one marriage in the Randall family. So many lives were about to be shattered. Yet by contrast, her own personal life was perhaps about to unfold into something heady and wonderful. Amy felt guilty for the thought amid disaster all around her.

After Amy left the homestead with Alex, he pulled over on the roadside in the police vehicle. Stephen couldn't know Amy was in town and since Alex probably held a greater degree of persuasion to set up a meeting, he phoned her brother. Annoyingly, his mobile went to voice-mail. He could do little more than leave a message to call him urgently.

Then at Amy's request, Alex phoned the Randall Transport office, only to be told by Stephen's PA, Jan, that he had travelled to Bendigo for a meeting with his father today.

Amy vaguely remembered mention of new planned developments being discussed at the last family conference, but she couldn't remember the date. Probably among all the other paperwork piling up and waiting in her cabin desk when she finally lived at home again. Damn. It was obviously today. Of all days!

Her only consolation was that at least if Stephen was in Bendigo he would be safe from Kelly.

Because Stephen's return call, when it came, would go to Alex, after he dropped Amy off back at his flat and went on call-outs and on patrol, he promised to let her know the moment he heard anything from her brother.

After spending an impatient wasted afternoon pacing indoors, it was late afternoon when Alex returned, and even later before Stephen phoned back. Alex put the call on speaker so Amy could listen in on the conversation.

'Hi, mate. What's the crisis?' Stephen asked wearily.

'I need to talk to you privately on Amy's behalf about this case she's working on. I'm afraid she made it sound important.'

'To who?' Stephen replied sharply.

Amy glanced at Alex. Damn. He was often grumpy after big official business meetings. He hated them. The cut and thrust; being the tough negotiator wasn't Stephen at all. Perhaps this one today hadn't gone well.

'Got time for a quick word before you go home, mate?'

'I should see Kelly first.'

No you shouldn't!

'Sure, I understand, but you couldn't swing by my flat on your way? Shouldn't take a minute.'

'No. After dinner. Maybe. Or in the morning.'

Stephen sounded like it had been a hard day and he didn't really care. Amy silently groaned. Tomorrow morning could be way too late.

'You can't make it sooner?' Alex pressed smoothly.

'Geez, mate, this better be important. Amy's pushing lately. I've had a long day. I'll try for later, okay?'

'Thanks, mate. Do your best. She'll appreciate

it. Oh, and Stephen? Still not a word to anyone about this, right? Amy's getting kind of paranoid.'

'Sure.' Stephen sighed and hung up.

'Sorry about the paranoid,' Alex apologised.

'That's okay. Whatever helps convince him.' Amy chewed her lip and frowned as she looked across at him. 'Alex, I'm scared.'

He stepped forward and gathered her in his arms. 'One hour at a time, okay?'

'I feel so helpless. We must be able to do something,' she moaned, her face pressed against his chest, her arms tight around him.

'Apart from storming around there, snapping on handcuffs and placing him under arrest, I don't see another way for now. We'll just have to wait.'

'He could be hours in that wicked woman's company.'

'I know,' he murmured, kissing the top of her head. 'Patience.'

'Oh please. Not my strong point.'

'He'll be fine.'

'We don't know that.'

'Have faith.'

He tilted up her face so their mouths and noses almost touched, then dipped just enough to kiss her. If he was aiming for a distraction, it helped.

As Alex stirred her blood, Amy wasn't short of an exciting idea as to how they could pass the time. But, anxious waiting for Stephen to appear, she knew she couldn't give Alex the full attention he deserved.

So they would just have to sit through this interminable hold-up. At least she was with Alex and not alone.

10

As Kelly Randall fussed in the kitchen and waited for Stephen's arrival, her gaze drifted to the wall calendar. This was the fourth day, and not a ripple of concern for the whereabouts of her sister-in-law, Amy. With each passing day, she grew increasingly confident of the woman's demise. She couldn't possibly have survived locked in the tunnel in this weather.

She needed to get the next stage rolling. Move along with her plan. Tonight would be perfect. Stephen would be weary from yet another important company meeting he disliked so much and therefore compliant.

First she would lower his defences with attention. Honestly, he was putty in her hands. Then she would pounce. She needed an increase in her already generous allowance to cover the mortgage repayments on this house. *Her* house, she preened, before the bank grew suspicious or Stephen even knew what she had done.

But only until she was a widow, when she would inherit all of Stephen's estate and be rich in her own right, deserving every cent. Able to write a cheque or sign any documents with the flourish of a pen.

The dream excited her. She was so close to success.

★　★　★

When Stephen Randall entered the townhouse, dropped his heavy briefcase on Kelly's gleaming tiled floor and loosened his tie, his wife as always soon appeared. She stood on tiptoe and kissed him, taking the tie and folding it neatly over a hook on the hall dresser.

He wasn't too tired to notice she still didn't seem herself lately. More unsettled and restless in recent days. He always nursed the impossible hope she might be pregnant, but even before marriage Kelly had told him she could not have children, so he had become reconciled to never being a father.

No. It was something else.

Strange that Alex had recently planted a seed of doubt about no relationship or family being perfect. He wondered if something was amiss in his own life and he had been too busy to notice.

When Kelly caught him staring at her, he cast a gentle smile over her fresh, cute face. 'Kelly, my sweet, you know if anything's troubling you, you can always confide in me.'

After a moment of mild alarm, she relaxed. 'You know me so well. There is a matter bothering me at the moment. I'll pour us a drink and we can talk about it before dinner.'

Reassured it was only a minor issue, Stephen watched his wife pour wine, bring over their glasses, and pat the seat beside her on the lounge for him to snuggle close as they often did before the evening meal. From their earliest married days, she made it plain his company business was never to be discussed at home.

Kelly held up her glass. 'To the future.'

Stephen clinked it and they each took a sip.

'I'm not sure how to say this, Stephen. I would simply hate for you to think less of me.'

'Of course I won't. You're everything to me. You know that.'

'That's partly my problem, you see.' She paused and flicked at an imaginary speck of lint on her tailored trousers. 'I feel like I am forever living in the Randall family shadow. Cora is so hardworking, and as your wife, I feel obliged to be the same. It can be quite demanding. I do feel as though I'm living my life just for you and the company.'

He understood, but before he could respond, she frowned. 'Do you not like the wine?' she asked, sipping her own and edging forward on the sofa beside him. 'It's a new label. I thought we might try it. If you prefer, I can open another bottle of your favourite — '

'No, no, my sweet, this is fine.'

When he took another long draught just to please her and his glass was almost empty, she seemed more at ease.

'I really didn't want to bother you with this after your long day but . . . ' She pushed out a shaky sigh.

'Go on,' he urged, focused intently on every word she said. She always hated asking him for anything.

'You're so dedicated to the business. Understandable of course,' she added quickly, 'and I appreciate your work is demanding, which all means that we hardly ever take time out for ourselves. I know we've travelled on company business together, both here in Australia and overseas, and it's been absolutely wonderful, my love.'

Stephen could never resist her sweet pleading. She was working toward something and it amused him. There was nothing he wouldn't do for her.

'I feel a *but* coming on,' he said cheekily, grinning. He finished his wine and she promptly topped it up.

'I know the company is hugely successful, and we've been married now for over three years, but caught up in the business all the time, I don't feel as if I'm an individual. Personally and . . . financially,' she pointed out carefully.

'Ah, my sweet. I've been so ignorant. Is that all that's bothering you?'

'Yes,' she said meekly. 'I'm so sorry to sound ungrateful, especially since I have my own car, we live in such comfort and have a strong marriage, it sickens me to even mention it. I could easily go out to work and earn a respectable living on my own account, but that would leave me hardly any time to devote to you and the company and still perform all our social obligations. Not to mention the charities your mother and I oversee and the committees we chair.'

Stephen shook his head. 'No, no. No need for you going out to work.' He yawned.

Kelly raised her arms in frustration 'And this is just an example, my love. You're exhausted.' She patted his knee and rose. 'Lie back and rest while I serve dinner. Just a small portion for you, and then we'll sort out whatever additional allowance you consider suitable for me but, after that, straight to bed.'

★   ★   ★

In the kitchen as she carefully sliced and plated up their salmon roulade with a crisp side salad and boiled baby potatoes, Kelly hummed with pleasure over her careful deception. A healthy crumble of Valium nicely dissolved into his wine did the trick. Despite their busy social life, Stephen's resistance to alcohol was low, so one full glass and the drug was enough to incapacitate and make him just drowsy enough to think he was naturally tired but still aware enough to do as she asked.

When she returned to the sitting room, he was dozing on the sofa. He sat up and ran a hand over his face.

'Too much wine, my love?' Kelly dutifully bustled off and reappeared with a glass of chilled water. 'I thought perhaps a nice red would help you relax. You left before eight for work this morning. You work far too hard. What's the point of your success if you don't stop to take time and enjoy it?'

She pulled his laptop closer and opened it. 'I can see you will be far too weary later, so how about we deal with this now before dinner, hmm?' She fondly stroked back the hair falling across his forehead.

'Good idea, my sweet. That new wine sure packs a punch.'

Kelly noticed he still wasn't fully aware yet. She always carefully phrased her appeals. Stephen usually agreed with everything she suggested or asked. Without question. He loved her deeply and without reservation. So sickly attentive, she despised him for that weakness alone. One of many.

'Then we can enjoy dinner at our leisure. And whatever comes after,' she said with soft suggestion, gently sliding her arms about his shoulders to kiss the skin beneath his ear as he typed, knowing the intimate action dissolved his resistance in the face of almost anything she wanted. And the gesture also enabled her to peek over his shoulder at the amount of her increase.

'Oh Stephen,' Kelly gasped, pretending surprise. 'Are you sure? That's incredibly generous.'

It was more than enough to manage the mortgage. This was just the start. With regular money of her own when Stephen was no longer in her life, she would inherit everything in his name and his share of the company.

If her husband hadn't been right beside her, she would have rubbed her hands together. With the money matter settled to her satisfaction, dinner progressed smoothly. Kelly expected she would only perform one more wifely duty, then carefully steer her final move into action.

So she was surprised and annoyed when Stephen rose immediately after the meal with no lingering over coffee as usual. She bristled at any change to her routine, especially without warning and no time to reorganise what she intended to do on this important night.

147

He frowned and ran a hand over his forehead. 'I've just remembered I need to duck out for a bit.'

'Oh Stephen, really.'

'It won't take long.' He kissed her cheek, preoccupied, his thoughts clearly already elsewhere. 'Alex wants me to drop around.' He hesitated and she sensed a hint of deception. 'To discuss some case he's . . . um . . . involved with.'

'You can't do it over the phone?'

'Apparently not.'

'Why not in the morning? We've barely had two hours together.'

Kelly pretended irritation because it meant her plan would be delayed until later tonight. Really, she wouldn't be living with him much longer, so what did she care?

'I've just realised Dad will want to go over our conference in Bendigo today first thing in the morning and debrief, so I'd better see Alex tonight.'

'Will you be late?'

'I expect not. Sorry, my sweet. Lots happening lately.'

'Text me before you return.'

She had risen from the table and sauntered to his side, pouting. His lingering kiss told her he would gladly stay. She longed to try her usual persuasion, but she needed to make her preparations.

'I'll be ready for you,' she growled.

'Witch,' he whispered. 'Be back soon.'

'Don't forget to text me.'

148

She needed warning to organise. Meticulous as always, she had carefully researched the dose but would add a little extra for good measure. She had managed her scheme perfectly so far. Nothing must go wrong or jeopardise this last step.

People overdosed on drugs all the time.

★ ★ ★

To Amy's relief, her brother sent a text he was coming around this evening after all. Before Stephen arrived, she mulled over the risk that he might hate and blame her for the rest of his life when he heard what she and Alex had to say. There was a strong chance that their brother-sister bond would be broken. But she couldn't dwell on that hurtful possibility because the Kelly issue was life and death.

She stayed in the flat so that when Stephen knocked, Alex met him at the door and the men trailed inside. At the first sight of him in days, knowing he was in one piece and safe, she almost wept with relief.

The instant he noticed her, Stephen beamed. 'Hey, sis. Back from your assignment?'

They shared a warm hug. 'I was doing research, but it wasn't for the *Gully Standard*. I've been in hiding.'

Stephen pulled back in shock. 'What on earth for? Must be serious stuff.'

Alex gave her a moment of reprieve before she began by drawing Stephen into the living area and indicating the sofa. 'You're not going to like

149

or even believe what you're about to hear, mate, but I swear it's the truth. We have proof. Amy will explain.'

An alarmed Stephen looked to his sister pacing nervously before him. 'I have some upsetting information about Kelly.' Amy closed then opened her eyes and shook her head. 'This will be hard, and there's no way I can prepare you for it.'

Stephen's mouth thinned. 'Spit it out. You and Kelly have never liked each other. Is this some kind of sour grapes or gossip?'

'No, Stephen. It's way beyond that.' Amy paused. 'We have reason to believe that Kelly may try to harm you.'

'Kelly? Harm *me*?' Stephen barked out an uncomfortable laugh. He glanced to Alex for support, then back at his sister. 'Amy, that's bullshit.'

Amy rubbed her arms and pushed on. 'Has Kelly said or done anything strange or different lately that seemed out of character?' The instant she noticed her brother give that familiar and slightly awkward lawyer hesitation, she guessed something had already happened. 'Stephen?' she pressed.

'I don't like to betray my wife behind her back. Kelly and I have always been open and honest with each other.'

'Stephen, this is no time to be loyal, and after what I have to tell you, you'll see it's not true. I have proof Kelly has deceived you. Big time.' It pained Amy to see the struggle on his face of a man caught between devotion and defensive

150

doubt. 'I swear anything you tell us will be in the strictest confidence.'

Stephen still wavered. 'It was only something small. I'm sure it's nothing.'

'What?'

'Kelly has always been humble and grateful for the comfortable life we lead.'

'She knows which side her bread is buttered,' Amy muttered.

'Ames,' Alex gently cautioned. 'Go on, Stephen.'

Reluctant, he admitted, 'Tonight she asked for an allowance increase.'

Amy and Alex glanced at each other. 'It's all about the money,' she whispered. 'She's building a nest egg, will do her worst with whatever she's planning, then disappear. Stephen — ' Amy crouched on the floor in front of him, pleading. ' — you must be careful. You're in very real danger.'

Stephen looked past his sister and addressed his mate. 'Alex, I can't believe you're a party to all this nonsense. Amy, you had no right to drag him into this accusation. You must be wrong.'

Amy slowly shook her head. 'We have proof.' It was time to tell him and, damn, this was going to hurt. 'Last Friday, Kelly contacted me to ask if we could meet at the cabin after I finished work. She wanted to meet me for a reason and with a certain intention in mind. When I got home, her car was around the back and she was inside waiting. With your pistol pointed straight at me.'

'What!'

'She forced me to drive my car to that old

mine tunnel in the bush reserve. She joined the local Historical Society this year, didn't she?' Amy didn't expect him to answer, just to get him thinking and process what she was about to say. 'They train their volunteers in taking the old gold tunnel tours, right? So she has access to a key to the locked gate entrance.'

'That doesn't mean — '

'Did you notice anything unusual about your pistol recently?'

Stephen looked anguished. 'She said she had been cleaning.'

'She forced me inside the tunnel at gunpoint and took two shots. The first one missed but the second one hit its mark.' Amy lifted up her sweater to show him the bullet wound in her shoulder.

'Kelly did that? This makes no sense. It can't be.'

It hurt Amy to see her brother still denying the truth.

'Why didn't you go to hospital? Report it?'

Perhaps seeing her emotionally struggling and to give her a breather, Alex entered the conversation. 'You can't force a person to report a crime unless they're willing, mate. It might have come down to Amy's word against Kelly's. She had the bullet graze, so Kelly would have been questioned. I recovered the shells from your pistol, but you had an alibi, so you're not implicated in any way. But you and I both know Ames, mate. Her reporter instinct kicked in. She needed to find some answers and the why. I couldn't tell her otherwise. But I've done an official full report every day on everything she's done to back her up.'

Amy ached to watch her brother's stunned expression turn to horror and his shoulders droop to hear all these revelations. 'I know it's a lot to take in, but we have witnesses. I passed in and out of consciousness during the night, but Augie Temple found me on Saturday morning. Said he heard moaning coming from the tunnel and thought it might be a wounded animal. I just said I'd had an accident and asked him to fmd Alex.'

'Mate?' Stephen appealed to his lifelong friend.

'I'm sorry, mate.' Alex stood astride, shaking his head. 'It happened exactly as Amy is telling you. The bullet was a deep graze, but she still lost a lot of blood overnight. Augie said she was injured, so I took a medical kit with me.'

'Stephen, I didn't tell Augie that it was Kelly. I've only told Alex. We three and Mum are the only ones who know Kelly is involved and guilty.'

Stephen's astonishment slowly turned to a building outrage. He bent forward, elbows on his knees and pushed both hands roughly up into his hair, lines of disbelief and agony distorting his face.

Amy's heart wrenched for his emotional pain. She wanted to ease it for him, but knew this was a journey and situation he must work through for himself. This news was not only the shattering of knowing a person and being betrayed, but when that person was a human

153

being you adored with every corner of your heart and life, it was a given the cut would go way deeper.

She sat down beside her brother, placed an arm across his shoulder and said softly, 'Before Kelly tried to kill me, she said *I was the first*. I have no idea who's next, but it's probably you, because other information has come to light to support what she's doing and why.'

Stephen's twisted expression was loaded with fury and his voice held an unfamiliar bitterness. 'I think she's already tried.'

'How?'

He explained about feeling drugged after the wine tonight before dinner. 'I can usually handle my wine. I only ever have one or two glasses. Kelly brushed away my concern by saying it was a new wine, hinting it might be stronger. It knocked me out for a bit, then she kept refilling my glass. We never do that. We always ask each other first. I thought that little action seemed off, too.'

Stephen's tone had taken on an air of defeat. From the devastation on his face, it was clear he was now adjusting to the truth of what Amy and Alex had told him. That his cherished wife was a fake.

They all sat quietly for a while, watching Stephen contemplate the layers of life as he knew it slowly peeling back and he now saw his perfect blissful marriage not with the glowing happiness of moments before but in the light of its new soured and crushing reality.

'I was conned! Used!'

Amy silently commiserated, for there was little left to say. They all needed time now to digest the oncoming upheaval that was about to affect all their lives. And Stephen would need more than the others, since the heartbreaking wreckage lay on his doorstep.

'This makes me feel so . . . so . . . ' Stephen gasped, unable to find the words.

'Just proves how set she was on revenge.'

Stephen waited a moment, then whirled on Amy. 'Why is she doing all this? What did you find out?'

'You up for the rest?' He nodded and sighed so she told him about Kelly's mother being alive. 'Her name is Helen Alice Simpson.'

Stephen twigged. 'The woman — '

'The one we asked you to look up in our company employment records.'

'*She's* Kelly's mother? She's *alive*?'

'She's in aged care in Maryborough. Kelly arranged to place her there. It's top-quality accommodation. Your financial affairs are your own business, and I don't want to know, but think on how Kelly could have managed that financially without your knowledge.'

Stephen frowned. 'The townhouse is in her name. Her allowance was generous. Even bigger now,' he scoffed, adding roughly, 'I'll be cancelling that. But even so, it's not enough to buy into a top complex like you've described. Kelly doesn't save. She spends. I didn't begrudge her that but — I suppose — Shit!'

Thin-lipped and glowering, he broke off and grabbed his phone. 'I'll call our bank manager

155

right now.' He pressed the number. 'Hey, Les. Stephen Randall,' he said brightly, an utter change of demeanour from seconds before.

Amy and Alex exchanged a glance. Her brother and his best mate was putting on a tough face, running on adrenalin to get himself through this.

'Apologies for the late call, Les,' he continued, 'but Kelly has just reluctantly told me about the mortgage on the house,' he chuckled. 'Said she didn't want to bother me. Just checking everything went through smoothly.' He paused and nodded, listening. Stephen laughed as though they were in league with one another. 'Yeah, Kelly is one astute woman, all right. It was to finance a business deal. I'll let you get back to your guests. Night, Les.'

He ended the call and threw his phone on the sofa in disgust. 'She mortgaged the house.'

Amy thought her brother's performance was masterful and was highly impressed. But behind the bleakness, his vacant gaze and thin mouth revealed the strain and effort it was taking to confront the truth, the extent of his wife's deception, and now the awakening as to how all the pieces fell into place.

'So we know how Kelly financed her mother's place in the institution,' Alex said quietly, 'but Amy has more on the Helen Simpson issue.'

Stephen grunted. 'Go on.'

'Tea, coffee, or alcohol first?' she asked.

'A beer would hit the spot,' Stephen said without emotion.

Alex fetched it while Amy sat beside him on

the sofa. When he had taken a deep drink, she continued.

'I saw Mum this morning to find out more information on Helen Simpson. See how much she remembered and knew. We've all watched Dad be generous in his attention to other women all his life. For the first time, although not in so many words, Mum basically admitted she suspected him of being unfaithful, but never asked.'

Amy waited a heartbeat, then voiced her incredible nagging fear. 'Since Helen Simpson was *dismissed*, we have no proof, but it's not impossible she was pregnant.'

Stephen stared at his sister. 'You saying because of Dad?'

Amy shrugged. 'Just putting it out there.'

'If that's the case, and Kelly is his daughter — ' He clamped a hand over his mouth.

The implication was too disastrous to consider. All three fell into a stunned silence.

Stephen broke it. 'I hate her!' he growled. 'I'm disgusted at who she is and what she's done. I hate her! I'm glad we never had kids.' He gave a short bitter laugh. 'That was probably another lie, too.' He upended his beer and gulped.

In the end, he finally crumbled. He bowed his head into his hands and quietly broke down, sobbing. He had always been man enough to show his emotions, but this shaking of his shoulders accompanied by loud cries of despair wrenched at his sister's heartstrings. She wished she could undo all that had happened, and go back four days when life might have taken a

157

different turn for them all. But it was too late.

Amy flung both arms about his neck and huddled against him, letting her own tears fall freely too. She was aware that Alex hovered beside them both, hands on hips, alternately pacing then growing still, his dark head thrown back to stare up helplessly at the white ceiling.

This whole episode had started decades ago by their father, his family now all suffering for his selfish substandard morals. The scandal about to break over the heads of the supposedly upstanding Randall family would rock Fossicker's Gully to its stony goldfield roots.

When Stephen's outpouring settled down, Alex took his empty beer can and thrust a shot of brandy at him. His mate took the glass and knocked it back in one gulp.

'One last problem,' Amy said. 'You can't go back to Kelly. It's too dangerous. But we can't alert her that I'm alive and you're onto her.'

'I'll spin a yarn. I often have sudden meetings. I can get away.' His hardened voice no longer held any emotion, his whole demeanour one of disturbing calm.

'You go home and pack some clothes,' Amy said. 'I'll give Alex my statement. Then, when you're done, swing back here and get me. Alex thinks we should go to my cabin, lock the doors, and stay out of sight. The police will take it from here.'

Amy and Alex had already decided not to leave Stephen alone.

'Once you two are safe,' Alex said, 'I'll go get Augie Temple and take his statement, too. Then by tomorrow morning, detectives will be in town. They'll be briefed and let us know how they want to play it.'

'I'd like all this to finish where it started,' Amy muttered. 'In the tunnel. See how Kelly likes it when the situation is reversed.'

Alex eyed her strangely.

★ ★ ★

When he arrived back home, Stephen ground his teeth, took a deep breath and stepped from his vehicle. He could do this. He wasn't afraid or angry. Neither feeling truly described how he felt. *Dead* was probably the best word. He winced at the pun.

He took the stairs two at a time and found Kelly reclining in bed, as he suspected. She *had* promised sex, but the thought now only made him sick.

'You kept me waiting,' she accused.

Now that he knew about the real Kelly Bates, her phony act turned his stomach. Once, her appeal would have set his pulse throbbing. Now he needed to hide his revulsion, pack and get out.

As he dragged his overnight bag from the walk-in robe, Kelly sprang up in bed, her filmy nightdress leaving nothing to the imagination.

'What are you doing?'

He tried to sound apologetic and disappointed. The lies came easily and without any sense of guilt. 'Dad phoned while I was with Alex. I need to get down to the city and bring

159

back a heap of important papers before our morning meeting.'

'That's ludicrous. What's wrong with an overnight courier?'

'The documents are highly private and sensitive.' He could no longer bring himself to add *my sweet*. She was nothing but a bitter taste in his life.

'You won't get any sleep.'

She probably hoped he crashed on the highway. Save her the trouble of whatever she had planned. Stephen threw a change of clothes and toiletries into his bag, zipped it up and eyed his wife with total indifference. He couldn't possibly kiss her.

'Sorry, Kelly.' He blew her a kiss. 'Looking like that, I daren't kiss you because I won't be able to resist you.'

'Then perhaps you shouldn't try,' she purred, suggestively squirming.

'I'll see you soon.'

He hoped not. He made one important stop in his office with the door closed and locked. Since his discussion with Alex and Amy, one thing had bothered him, so with careful modifications he fixed it.

He shrugged on his overcoat, filled his pockets, and left the house for what he presumed was probably the last time.

★ ★ ★

Kelly Randall glowered in fury at her husband's back as he left. This was not meant to happen.

Being forced to wait yet another twenty-four hours was infuriating.

Frustrated, and feeling excited with the impending thoughts of wealth and freedom, she grew lustful and spread her legs to pleasure herself. As she shuddered with climax and grew calmer, she decided if there were any more delays in carrying out her husband's demise, she would simply leave and divorce him.

Half of everything was a poor second prize, but growing desperate and impatient, it was an option she was prepared to consider to escape this dump of a town, which, to be fair, had been a start.

There would be other targets out there in the future, as easily charmed and even richer, just ripe for picking.

And she would find them.

11

The moment her daughter left, Cora Randall wandered into the glorious sun-drenched conservatory overlooking the landscaped rear gardens of Windarrah.

As gracious and commanding as the Randall family property had always been, filled with half a lifetime of memories, both pleasant and unfortunate, the lady of the house crossed her arms and reflected at length on the news Amy had brought today.

Shocking enough about Kelly and alarming about her husband, yet knowing the man she had married, not unsurprising. She was consumed by a fierce sense of disappointment in herself for enduring her unhappy situation, and outrage at the sordid extent of her husband's indiscretions, so it only took moments to make two necessary decisions.

A telephone call to arrange an appointment, and the other matter would just have to wait for David's return.

It proved a long day, but eventually her husband returned. To no dinner and, except for the flickering electric fire, a house in virtual darkness, his wife sitting in her favourite drawing-room recliner.

David Randall strode into the room. 'Aren't you well?'

'I'm perfectly fine. Thank you for asking. Not usually your habit.'

'What's going on?'

Cora patiently related the gist of Amy's conversation and disclosure about their criminal daughter-in-law.

'Kelly?' David barked in disbelief.

'We knew little enough of her background, and didn't probe because she said her father was never in her life and her mother had already died. When she is, in fact, very much alive and living in Maryborough. I believe you knew her.'

He scoffed. 'Impossible.'

'Actually, it's not. I haven't told you who she is. Her name is Helen Simpson.'

David started in surprise, an expression of fear slowly moving across his handsome face. The Randalls were still an elegant couple, the passing years so far treating them both kindly. The district's social elite.

'She was dismissed. Being her boss, you will know why, although you never told me.'

'You didn't ask.'

Cora sent her husband a challenging glare as he slowly sank onto the sofa opposite in this, the grandest and her favourite of all Windarrah's rooms. She would miss it. David looked quite ill with a dawning realisation. She knew he would try and talk his way out of any responsibility, so she needed to be blunt.

'Was she pregnant by you?'

'Cora, that was years ago — '

'But you remember as though it was yesterday,' she countered, daring him to lie.

He blustered. 'She approached me.'

'And you gave her your fullest attention.'

163

He paused. 'I know it was weak of me but — the woman flirted,' he sneered. He looked aside and mumbled, 'She was — willing.'

'Never an excuse, David. More importantly, you were married to me at the time. Besides,' she added quietly, 'it's not always the female at fault, and I believe *the woman* has a name. I will be seeking a divorce.'

'That's an overreaction,' he joked in disdain, his ego lashed. 'A bit drastic.'

'Not after a lifetime of infidelity, no.'

'Cora, dear, there's no need to go that far. This will all blow over. We're too important in town for gossip to last.'

Cora grinned to herself. 'You're not important, David. You're only endured because you pour money into the community. I no longer care to be exposed to your pompous attitude and low standards.'

He lowered his voice and shifted in his chair as he cajoled, 'I admit, I've not been as attentive and the best husband I could be, but I've built up a million-dollar business. I'm a wealthy man, Cora, and I've always been prepared to share that with you.'

'How generous.' Cora smiled sadly to herself as he preened, so ignorant that he believed her comment a compliment and not sarcasm. 'At the expense of any quality in your family life, of course.'

David attempted to reach out and come closer but Cora held up a hand, rose and drew away. 'I'll be moving out. Now.'

'And leave our beautiful home?' he mocked.

It was beautiful and, cruelly, she did love it, but her life needed to change. 'It's not a home, David. To me, as the years have passed, it has never felt more than a cold prison.'

'Surrounded by all this luxury?' Only appearances mattered to this shallow man. 'You have nowhere else to go.'

'No, at the moment I haven't the faintest idea, but I'm sure something will occur to me.' Which was a lie, because she already had accommodation booked indefinitely from tonight. But she enjoyed a little tease anyway, allowing the innate humour she usually suppressed to finally escape. 'I know both my son and daughter would welcome me with open arms, but I prefer to be independent.'

She needed him to see she didn't care and that she was now her own person, as she should have been years ago.

'You won't survive alone.'

'Such pessimism. If I can survive living with you for over thirty years, I can do anything,' she announced calmly, although inwardly seething with her hands tightly clasped together to stop their shaking.

'Old Bernie won't represent you,' he snapped. 'Conflict of interest. He does all my business.'

Cora knew this meant that David felt he owned the only local ageing town solicitor, the extremely tolerant Bernard Slater, merely because he entrusted all company matters to his firm.

'I don't need him, David. I have already engaged my own lawyer.

'Who?'

165

She glared at him and shook her head in frustration. Honestly, the man was so thick. 'My son.'

Cora deliberately did not mention him as being *their* son. It didn't need a senior's best guess to know that when the scandal broke, Stephen would abandon the company quicker than he could snap his fingers.

'You've contacted Stephen already?'

'Obviously. In one year and a day, we will be divorced. In the meantime, there will be no contact between us, so I want all negotiations to be directed solely through him.'

Cora was quite enjoying this. She would become a wealthy woman, but her haste to leave was filled with regret, remaining blindly apathetic for so long, waiting for a catalyst when she should have taken the lead and walked out years ago.

She turned her back on the man for whom she now only held contempt and had done for many years of their married life. With a light step, Cora trotted towards her packed suitcases on the front porch. Almost as an afterthought, she turned to face the stunned lost man still standing in the middle of their elegant room.

'Selma Hammond comes on Thursdays. After she cleans, she'll change the linen and towels and do any washing you leave in the laundry hamper. There's some food in the refrigerator, or you may prefer to eat at the pub.' She deliberately chose that word over *hotel* because, snob that he was, David hated its use. 'Please yourself.' She smiled. 'You always do. Oh . . . ' She hesitated.

' . . . one other thing. You need to tell your children about their grandfather. If you don't, I will.'

'Why?'

'Honestly, David, for a big company boss, sometimes you can be so dense.'

And with that she turned away again, having already phoned for a taxi. With perfect timing, its headlights even now beamed down the driveway toward the house.

★   ★   ★

Before midnight, teams of detectives and support police had descended on Fossicker's Gully, their vehicles amassed around the small country station.

Amy had given a full report and been interviewed at length. Augie Temple had also been brought into the station and willingly made a statement, too. By coincidence, they met in passing along the station corridor, the small building bustling with police.

'How ya doin', lass?' The old gold fossicker looked at her strangely with longing fondness.

Thinking it was because he had found and saved her, she stopped and smiled warmly to reassure him. 'I'm fine. I'm healing. Physically, anyway. The other stuff might take a bit longer. It all seems so unreal.'

Augie was escorted back to his shack in the scrub in a police vehicle, Amy and Stephen bundled into another to be transported to the safety of her cabin under police guard.

Throughout the night, for no one slept, Alex sent texts and made phone calls to keep them updated on all developments. Naturally there had been a long and thorough briefing on the attempted murder.

The pistol bullets and Alex's photographs of Amy's bullet wound, together with all involved witness statements and his daily official police record of the last four days' events, all became vital evidence.

Amy was filled with an unreal sense of loss because she no longer had control of the situation, yet knew with both the deepest tension and reprieve that the next step was in the capable hands of the law.

Alex's last phone call, before she and Stephen headed for bed in the cabin, exhausted by the early morning hours, held a surprising development.

'The suspect,' he explained as she wearily sprawled on the cabin sofa, her mobile on speaker so Stephen could listen, 'is often tempted out of curiosity to return to the scene of the crime. I ran your comment past the detectives. About wishing Kelly's apprehension could be in the tunnel, so they're setting up a sting there in the morning.'

'Really?' Amy livened up a little with excitement. To her mind, rather than a simple arrest, the woman deserved to be taunted to the location of her crime by its failure. Amy's survival. 'So who's the bait?' she innocently asked.

Alex fell silent on the other end for a moment. 'You.'

Amy grew chilled. 'Oh.'

'Only if you agree.' While Amy hesitated, he added, 'You'll be quite safe and protected at all times.'

'I know. All right.'

'Better get a good night's sleep.'

'Right.'

'Kelly will be enticed to the tunnel. If she shows up, it will seal her guilt.'

Amy didn't ask about details. At this point she chose not to know. Time enough for that tomorrow. For now, she and Stephen were taking one hour at a time.

'Now that Stephen's safely out of the house, we've set up surveillance on her. I'll keep you posted on her movements after that. I'll text you as soon as the Melbourne guys are ready to roll. They'll come by the cabin to prepare you for the meeting in the tunnel. You as the victim, and Stephen as the suspect's husband, will be the only members of the public allowed into the tunnel and involved with the operation.'

'Okay.'

'Ames,' he said softly, 'everything will be fine. I'll be there in the background.'

'You better be.'

'Promise,' he murmured.

She hugged the affection in his deep voice to herself for comfort. Facing Kelly would be the hardest thing she had ever done in her life, but this encounter was for Stephen. She could do it.

'Thanks. Night.'

Amy and Stephen hugged each other, few words spoken between them, both needing sleep, if only a few hours, keen for the following morning to come and the sting to get underway.

'You okay?' Amy asked her brother as they walked upstairs together, arms linked.

'Fine. Just want it all to be over, you know?'

★ ★ ★

At barely daylight next morning, Amy and Stephen were woken by the first detectives to arrive at the cabin. Somehow sister and brother forced down breakfast while the officers briefed them on the strict sequence of events and protocols to go down.

They were not to deviate in any way, do strictly as told, and were assured with the full confidence of an efficient tactical team that all would be well.

Stephen paced. Amy practised deep breathing ahead of returning to the cold, dark tunnel to face the woman who tried to kill her.

Too soon, everyone heard the police radio blare into life. 'She's on her way.'

Amy's heart pounded in dread and she stiffened to prepare herself for the ordeal to come. Before she walked into the tunnel, she looked around for Alex nearby, reassured. He smiled then she saw him reach for his mobile, an expression of alarm crossing his face as he talked. He anxiously glanced back in her direction but walked off toward his vehicle.

Where the hell was he going at a time like this? What was wrong?

Amy didn't have time to dwell on possible

170

answers to all the questions racing through her mind, because an officer grabbed her arm to lead her into position.

The sting was on.

★ ★ ★

Kelly Randall sipped her first cup of tea after breakfast, calm in the face of Stephen's return today and the magnitude of what she had planned. To be disturbed by the front doorbell at this hour was the height of irritation.

She hurriedly signed for the small sealed envelope personally addressed to her, since the postman seemed edgy and keen to move on.

It all seemed rather mysterious, since there was no stamp or postmark. A private local delivery? From who? Perhaps something to do with one of her town committees. She frowned on her way back to the breakfast room, slit open the flap, and withdrew a single sheet of paper.

'*I know what you did. Meet me there now.*'

Kelly froze for a moment, then fury rose up from within at this surprise demand. Who had found out what she'd done, and how? She had covered her tracks and accomplished her plan to perfection.

This sudden disruption was aggravating in itself, throwing her day and scheme into chaos.

She ran upstairs, dressed warmly against the outdoor chill to come, which included a thick pair of gloves as a precaution, and made a brief stop in Stephen's office on the way down. The

171

tunnel gate key was on the keyring in her shoulder bag.

Blast this disorder.

Kelly backed from the garage with a discreet glance up and down the street. Apart from one or two extra cars parked further along, all seemed normal.

She headed south and drove to the tunnel. When she pulled up, she looked around, scanning the surrounding bushland. No one, no movement. Utter silence. She expected someone would meet her outside or near the mine.

With her every sense on alert, she shoved the gun deep into her coat pocket and emerged from her vehicle to venture away from the car, strolling warily closer to the tunnel gate.

There had been no tours lately in the mine, so no one from the Historical Society would have accessed it. Who among them could possibly know about last Friday? Apart from society members and the local council staff, no one else held keys or would be likely to need access. As winter drew closer, mine tours were suspended until spring. A major factor why Kelly chose this time of year to take action.

Clearly she was early. She waited and paced for ten minutes, growing edgier as each one passed. Was it a hoax? No. This was too real and deliberate. Perhaps her cowardly blackmailer wouldn't show. Whoever it was would not outfox her. Despite the unexpected note and haste to appear, she had her wits and a weapon.

Her craving to investigate the tunnel peaked like an addiction she could not break, fuelled by anger that she might have to leave town in haste sooner than expected. Hardly a chore escaping from this wretched boring country town, but at least she would escape with more than she ever dreamed.

Once she had dealt with this morning's little hiccup, she would continue as planned. Eager yet afraid to find the corpse inside, Kelly sharpened her attention, her shoes crunching on the stony ground.

With excited trembling hands, Kelly turned her key in the padlock and pulled the gate ajar. With her weapon drawn from her pocket and pointed ahead, both hands wrapped firmly around it, she cautiously crept down the tunnel, coldly confident in her own ability to deal with this unexpected crisis. Having killed once, she would do it again.

She stopped short, shock waves tearing through her body, to see Amy Randall standing before her. Very much alive.

12

Alex sped away from the mine-tunnel sting, torn between his strong need to be with Amy and a phone call that promised family trouble. His bloody old man was out of gaol and home.

He'd had seconds to weigh up the risks of both. Honestly, Amy was more than protected and covered for any eventuality. Detectives, plain-clothes and boys in blue, were everywhere in the bush and tunnel, trained and ready to pounce. Whereas his ma, Selma, was probably alone and needing his support.

Since this was the first time Jim Hammond was in town as a free man with his son as the local cop, he also wanted to take the opportunity of a few words.

As he pulled up in front of the old place, his useless brother Buddy's clapped-out old wreck of a sedan was parked in what served as the driveway along one side of the house. And he was just getting out of the car with Jim.

Why the hell wasn't Buddy at work? Took the day off to get their notorious father from prison? Alex would have let the old man walk.

As the oldest Hammond kid as he grew up, Alex became a wary loner, flinching away from his father, the man who was supposed to set an example for the family, not be its disgrace.

His memories as a boy were of the police always being called, sometimes the need for an ambulance, and his mother ending up in hospital, first responder vehicle lights flashing out the front of their house in the street. His whole childhood one big mash up of violence, upheaval and, as he grew, watching out for his younger brothers and sisters, but especially Selma.

By his teens, taller and stronger than Jim, seeing the wrong and imbalance of power over and disrespect for his mother, Alex began quietly standing beside her, his fear having turned to anger, drawing scorn and rage from his father, drunk or sober.

Being unable to turn his oldest son to a life of crime, Jim took Buddy under his wing, a rebel from the start. These days, Alex suspected, he was moving from petty crime to much worse. Now that he had returned to Fossicker's Gully as the town's cop, he could officially protect his two sisters and young Billy, too easily influenced, just deciding which path to take in life. Taunted and challenged by Jim and Buddy to be a man and toughen up. So far Billy had weakened but not given in and joined them. Alex planned to see it stayed that way and his little brother on course for something better.

Now, Jim Hammond sneered as his oldest son strolled forward looking official and smart in uniform. 'They told me you was a cop.' He spat on the ground at his son's feet.

'They were right,' Alex drawled. He briefly nodded in Buddy's direction, then returned his focus to his father and said with unflinching quiet warning, 'You so much as raise your voice to my mother or lay one finger on that God-fearing hardworking woman and you'll answer to me. I'll report every single act of abuse you were ever responsible for. Don't forget I witnessed every one of them. And if you run like the coward you are, I'll hunt you down, put you away and lose the key.'

'How you gonna do that, boy?' he cackled.

'You're eyesight's failing, Jim. I'm a man now, not a defenceless boy you can use as a punching bag. Just a timely warning that I'll be watching you. One foot wrong, understand?'

Wiry old Jim Hammond had grown gaunt with age this past decade and didn't look quite so formidable. Alex sensed he was likely all bluster these days.

'A badge and a uniform and that fancy police car don't make you better than us.'

'Don't claim to be, and this badge and uniform can put you back in prison. Is that where you want to be? Doesn't look like your latest stay has treated you well. Think on your life, Jim, and try to make a change.'

It sickened him to say it, but Alex added, 'More than willing to help if you need it. Starting with giving up the drink and working on controlling your fists and temper. Either way, I don't give a damn. You can go right back through the turnstile and inside again. Your choice.'

Alex had said his piece. As a policeman with the law on his side and as a son.

Edgy with thoughts of the mine tunnel sting going down without him when he had promised

Amy he would be there for her, while he wasted time on a pathetic human being, Alex strode indoors to his mother, surprised to see both his sisters in the kitchen at her side.

'Lisa. Julie.' He greeted and hugged each one. 'Thanks for being here for Selma. Hey, little Gracie.' He kissed the soft blonde curly locks of his niece's head as she sat on her grandmother's knee. 'Ma.' He bent and squeezed her tight.

His father and brother trailed like awkward strangers into the house. Buddy lived with a houseful of dodgy mates, all of them under Alex's personal and police scrutiny. And Jim was still at home because Selma was too goodhearted to throw him out.

'James,' his mother greeted her husband. 'You'll be in the sleepout off the veranda. Lisa and Gracie are moving into the spare room, so no smoking or drinking in this house around my grandchild.'

Alex's eyebrows rose and he privately grinned in the deepest respect for his mother's apparent new house rules. Maybe she *had* taken on board a little of what they discussed recently. *This* was why Alex had returned. In the hope, if they all pulled together, he could help make changes happen for his family.

Jim's reaction throughout was unspoken belligerence. They would all still have to watch him, but it looked like the old bloke was wearing out.

Feeling way more positive than when he arrived, Alex said, 'Time this family shaped up. Ma — ' He laid a hand on her shoulder and she gripped it firmly. ' — this time we're all here for you, and I need to know.' She nodded her understanding. 'The bad stuff stops now. You girls,' he addressed his sisters, 'pleased to see you both watching out for your mother.'

'Thanks, bro.' Julie grinned.

'Proud to be here,' Lisa said with a new strength Alex hadn't seen before, clearly lending her courage.

'I need to get back to the salon, Ma,' Julie said. 'See you later. Pa. Buddy.' She barely acknowledged them as she brushed past on her way out.

Aware of time ticking by, Alex wanted to stay longer but knew he also wanted to be there for Amy. Since all seemed under his ma's determined control now, he made his departure, trying not to break the town speed limit back to the mine tunnel.

★ ★ ★

'What's wrong, Kelly? Seen a ghost?' Amy was ecstatic to see her sister-in-law halt in shock before the scheming woman assumed her icy controlled mask once again.

'So,' she sneered, 'I missed you last time. Not today.'

Amy closed her eyes as she watched Kelly squeeze the trigger on the raised gun. A bright flash and the sound of an explosion burst around the tunnel. The blank fired with no bullet. Clever Stephen. A murderer's mistake. Not checking the weapon.

With shock and outrage sweeping across her pained face, Kelly tried again and again.

Amy sank against the tunnel wall with relief, grateful for the flak jacket beneath her windcheater. Stephen had filled his gun with blanks and removed all ammunition from the townhouse in his coat pockets last night before he left.

With daylight behind him, only Amy could see the shadowed body of a familiar man so dear to her walk slowly into the tunnel. His footsteps crunched on the loose stones that littered the tunnel floor.

At the sound, Kelly whirled around and gasped. 'Stephen!'

'We removed the bullets. *My sweet.*' His devastated trembling voice was spiked with bitterness.

Amy's heart ached for him. Her brother's face was haggard with a desolation his distraught sister thought he might never overcome. Neither of them had deserved this.

Then Amy's heart filled with a deep sweetness and passion as Alex appeared at the tunnel entrance beyond. She thought he silently mouthed the words *I love you* but, with the distance, she wasn't sure. She smiled and cried at the same time. Relieved and sad and happy all at once.

'You okay, sis?' Stephen whispered, sliding his arm around her shoulder.

'I'm fine. Now.'

Then men and women of the Force appeared from everywhere to surround Kelly, but held back and did not approach or interfere as the tunnel was suddenly floodlit from all sides.

Kelly glared at Amy and Stephen, horror at being trapped and caught sweeping across her contorted face. 'Their father is to blame, not me.' Her frantic yelling bounced off the walls.

'Why?' Stephen growled as sister and brother clung to each other.

'He left my mother pregnant and sacked her with only a few measly dollars for an abortion. She didn't have it. She needed the money instead. That baby, my sister, got sick and died. I wanted your family to know what it's like to lose a child.' Her screaming voice shook with rage. 'My mother took any job she could get. Dragged herself up with nice clothes, shoes and guts. Leered at by fat cats in suits by day and lying on her back at night for a few extra bucks. We lived tough while you wealthy bastards lived like kings.'

Suddenly, totally out of character, Stephen reached out and slapped his wife's face.

'How dare you!' Kelly bellowed in outraged offence, cringing and pressing a hand to her cheek as though she bore no fault for any of this.

'No,' he replied quietly, 'how dare *you*.'

The sting team closed in. Alex, Amy and Stephen watched as Kelly was arrested and handcuffed, her face red with fury, eyes wild. Then, like the mates they had always been, the childhood trio turned their backs on her and walked away together out into the weak autumn morning sunlight.

Outside, ignoring the official police activity

around them, Alex grabbed Amy in a fierce hug, kissing her hair, her cheeks, smothering her with affection so she could barely breathe, and loved it. She chuckled, lapping it up, knowing there was so much more ahead for them.

He groaned, 'I'll be tied up at the station for a while.'

'And I need to head down to the *Standard* office to warn the guys what's coming. This will hit the news in hours and the media will be swarming all over town.'

'Catch up soon.' He kissed her with longing.

'Please,' she whispered, hating that they must break apart again.

As Alex strode away, swept up in the police aftermath of the sting, as much as Amy had loved living with him and had no doubt he was her future, for now she longed simply to know the peace and solitude of her cabin in the bush. Home.

She and Alex certainly had no privacy in their emotional reunion, all safe in the knowledge that their ordeal this past week was finally over. Stephen had given them space amid the surrounding action and caught up with her before they left.

'How are *you* doing?' Amy asked.

'Pushing through.'

'I need to head down to the paper now, but I'll phone Mum to meet at the cabin soon. We all need to chat and reflect. Wanna come?'

He nodded. 'Great idea.'

They hugged and parted.

13

For Amy, the simple habit of jumping into her car again was bliss. Being outdoors without fear or looking over her shoulder, independent. It was fabulous to be alive. Main Street hadn't changed in the last twenty-four hours, she noted, cruising slowly along, savouring its familiarity, except for the fleet of police vehicles around the station. She parked in front of the *Gully Standard* office and strode inside.

At the front desk, Georgia leapt to her feet. 'You're back!'

Michael spun around in his swivel chair across the room. 'Where the hell have you been?'

'Don't complain. I bet you loved being boss.'

'You look like shit.' He frowned.

'Thanks.'

Georgia intervened excitedly, 'There's something happening in the Gully for a change. Did you see all the cops? Michael thinks — '

Amy held up a hand. 'I can tell you all about it. Michael, you still keep that bottle of whiskey in your bottom drawer?'

He had the honesty to blush. 'Yep.'

'Okay, Georgia, pour three shots into our kitchen glasses. We need to talk. Michael, you'll want to record this.'

Jaws dropped and gasps from her colleagues punctuated Amy's recounting of the past days' events, focusing strictly on facts and details.

Then she outlined what she expected from each of them professionally. Michael couldn't hide his delight at being given a decent lead story for a change and the potential boost to his career. Georgia listened, embracing it all but with far more empathy.

Although it was at the expense of her family, Amy knew an honest unbiased account of Kelly's crime needed to be reported. 'Without sensation, okay?' Amy eyeballed Michael.

'Sure.'

'Georgia, you'll be front line on the phone and for whoever walks through the door. I know you've got this, but when the media descend, think before you speak. Firm and professional at all times, okay?'

The girl gave a thumbs-up. 'Check.'

Georgia was still young, but Amy knew this story would only add to her experience and she would learn on the go.

'Right,' Amy said, 'I'm taking the rest of the day off. Call me with any issues or questions.'

Driving out to the cabin past the police station humming with vehicles and cops, this time for at least twenty-four hours, Amy hoped to physically and emotionally revive. She couldn't wait to just stand still and breathe.

She called her mother on speaker from the car. 'It's all over, Mum. I'm almost at the cabin. Wanna join me?'

'That's such a relief. I've been so worried. Of course I'll pop over, dear. Have you eaten anything?'

'I had a light breakfast.'

'I'll bring food.'

'And wine.'

'Gotcha.'

'Stephen's coming too.'

'See you both soon then, dear.'

Amy presumed her father would be in the office as usual. Everything stopped for his work. At some point, she and Stephen needed to have a conversation with him. Not today. They all deserved time to rally and recover. Gather thoughts, each process what had happened and put steps in place to move forward.

Down the track there would be Kelly's court case and trial in Melbourne. She would deal with that when it arose. For now, the Randalls needed to unite and draw strength from each other.

Amy's thoughts went to a certain irresistible guy she had adored from afar all her life. She would prefer *that* reunion to be private. When Kelly was taken away and the city cops left, he would be free. She couldn't wait but knew she must.

Back in her cabin, Amy lit the open fire, immediately making it feel like home. Just as well, because her mother breezed through the back door soon after.

'Did I see you arrive in a taxi?'

'Yes, dear.'

'Where's Cecil? Having the night off?'

'Something like that.' Her mother sounded evasive. 'Stephen not here yet?'

That was obvious. She was making small talk. Something was up. 'No. He sounded like he would be right over but must have been held up.'

Dressed in fitted jeans, low heels and a long designer cardigan, a pastel scarf draped around her neck, Cora was still youthful and attractive in her fifties, her short wavy hair softly framing her face. This gracious lady had readily hovered in the background of all their lives, supporting without question or complaint. And tonight positively glowed. Relieved that her husband's disloyalty was finally exposed? Amy wondered. She looked like a new woman.

Her daughter had assumed, wrongly as it was immediately obvious, that she would need to support her mother through this time of family upheaval, but Cora Randall had miraculously and promptly gathered her wits with a determination and strength that had probably been there all along but no one had noticed and she had never allowed to sparkle.

Cora had entered bearing a bulging bag of food and an equally heavy one clinking with bottles of wine. 'Wow, bet the IGA welcomed you today.'

Her mother began unpacking cheeses, olives, salami, dips and more onto the bench, then moved into the kitchen to chop up fruits and dipping vegetables. 'I'll find my way around. You go and soak in a bath.'

Speechless at her mother's positive transformation, Amy didn't need convincing. When she returned downstairs later in a comfy tracksuit and thick wool socks, Cora had a platter of nibbles set out on the small living-room table, glasses of wine already poured. Always the efficient homemaker, Amy grinned to herself. It

185

didn't matter that she was an adult now, she loved being looked after for a change.

'Now sit down and tell me everything,' Cora said.

Amy gratefully offloaded about this morning's sting and Kelly's arrest. 'It was terrifying facing her and having the same gun pointed at me again.'

'I can't begin to imagine,' Cora murmured.

Then Stephen pulled up outside. 'Sorry I'm a bit late. Stopped at the townhouse and packed my things. Can you believe it almost fits in the four-wheel drive?'

Amy saw through the bright front and sent him a concerned glance.

He hugged his mother, then perched on the end of the sofa and laid a reassuring hand on his sister's shoulder. 'I'm okay. I'm not going back. I want nothing more to do with that place. Divorce is a given.'

Amy admired his outward show of strength and made a toast. 'To a better future for all of us.'

With everyone relaxed from food and wine, and warm before the crackling fire, Stephen rose and moved over to rest an elbow on the mantelpiece, a glass of wine in the other hand, staring down into the flames.

'We all have news, so I'll go first. Amy, thanks for letting me stay here, but because it's the centre of town, I've booked, can you believe, the honeymoon suite at the pub.'

Amy groaned with irony.

Stephen shrugged. 'It's big and grand and has

186

its own bathroom. Besides, they do the best steaks in town. With a glass of beer, a roof over my head and a bed for the night, I'll be set. Just until I find a new place.'

'You know you can stay here as long as you want.'

'I know.' He sent her a knowing smile. 'But you need your privacy.'

Amy felt herself blush. 'The offer stands,' she murmured.

'I appreciate it. Because my ex is heading to prison and the house is in her name, the mortgage payments she set up from her own account will lapse, so in default, the property will be put up for sale. I'll grab what furniture I need and put it into storage.'

He glanced across at his mother, drained his wine and accepted a refill. 'I'll be leaving the company but staying in the Gully. Time for a change on all fronts. I was growing dissatisfied anyway. I want to get back to practising law. I've already set up an appointment with Bernie Slater to discuss joining his legal firm until he retires in a few years. I've heard rumours and watched him slowing down.'

'Awkward for Dad,' Amy quipped. 'Will you take on the Randall Transport company business?'

'If I buy out Bernie, I inherit his clients.'

'You're even sounding like a lawyer again already,' Amy chuckled.

Despite his upbeat plans for his new future, Amy was sure Stephen's outer bravado hid struggles beneath. He was still young. He would move on emotionally eventually, but he had been so deeply in love and devoted to Kelly it would take a while, and he would probably be wary. Amy prayed that in time, he found a genuine love.

She was absolutely on board in being there for her brother. They would all take care of each other. Fallout was inevitable, which she was sure would take many forms, since everyone's lives had been so deeply affected, more or less a complete Randall family disintegration.

'Well, I've made some changes too, as you would both imagine,' their mother said. 'Not everything remains the same as it has always been, as we have all discovered.'

'Of course.' Amy wondered what was coming.

'I've been aware of your father's . . . behaviour,' she announced carefully, 'for years. This latest eruption hasn't just affected me, though, has it? So I've decided to walk away with my dignity and my head held high. Permanently.'

Stephen didn't seem surprised, but Amy's gaze popped as Cora smiled softly and raised her glass. 'To divorce, finally demanding the respect I deserve, walking away with a share of a transport empire and allowing the cause for women's equality to take a tiny step forward.'

'Mother!' Amy darted her gaze toward her brother.

'He knows. I left Windarrah last night and I have already engaged him as my lawyer,' she announced proudly, grinning at her son.

'Well. Way to go, Mum.' Amy leaned forward on the sofa and high-fived her mother.

'I'm actually looking forward to the sparks and fire,' Cora chuckled, looking glamorous and positive while her life of over thirty years crumbled around her.

'I believe I'll enjoy it as much as you,' Stephen admitted soberly.

In that moment, holding back tears for all the drama of recent days, Amy hoped at some appropriate point in this gem of a woman's future that another kinder, appreciative partner entered her mother's life for laughter and companionship.

Of course she hoped it for Stephen, too, but Amy suspected her brother's road to healing would take longer.

Cora said quickly, 'I don't need a bed. I'm booked into Molly's B&B. Indefinitely.' She glanced between them and grinned. 'I'm going to have to learn to drive! I'm looking forward to getting behind the wheel of my own car.' Her forehead wrinkled with a frown. 'I'm afraid Cecil will be out of a job.'

Because Windarrah was situated on vast acres on the edge of town, David had always provided a car and a driver, one of his retired employees, for his unlicensed wife.

'Dad will be lost living out there in that big house alone,' Amy reflected, sipping wine and staring into the fire.

Through an inflated sense of his own worth and importance, David Randall had caused his own downfall. She knew the divorce would hurt him far more than her mother. For loss of prestige alone.

189

Okay, so he wasn't a perfect human being. Who was? And he was still her father. She would always be polite and have him in her life. Distantly, perhaps, until the current family turmoil eased.

Amy sighed. New endings and beginnings were ahead for them all.

By early afternoon, Stephen was the first to make a move and leave. He hugged and kissed his mother and sister, and left to move into the pub and see Bernie Slater.

Cora lingered a while longer. The women wound up their chat with coffee and chocolates.

As Amy licked peppermint cream filling off her fingers, she said, 'I want to go and see Augie Temple. Being in hiding, I've had no chance to personally thank him for finding me and saving my life.'

'He's a lovely old man.'

Amy was surprised to hear her mother say so with such affection. 'You know him?'

'As much as he will allow anyone to get close to him. You'll learn a lot from him. Ask him why he lives like a bush hermit.'

'Actually, I might.' Amy was encouraged by her mother's interest and local knowledge. 'Augie's clearly a private soul, but he was an important first part of all the disruption in recent days. It started me thinking about my aspiration to write a book and the demographic of older people in town. There must be heaps of other older residents with interesting stories and lives.'

'Old Eddie Ryan was a National Service conscript in the Sixties. He was sent to Vietnam and fought in the war. But not every soldier wants to talk about their experiences. You'd need to tread carefully there.'

'I'll keep him in mind.'

'And Selma was in the theatre. Or was it a circus?' She frowned. 'Anyway, her troupe travelled around the country, and that's how she met Jim.'

'Really? I must ask Alex.' Amy reflected on how little she *really* knew about people in town. Such a treasure of stories out there just waiting to be told. 'With each person's approval, of course, I'd love to do a series in the *Standard* and maybe later combine them into a sort of local history book.'

'Sounds a wonderful project, dear.'

Amy loved how her mother was so supportive of her children. In contrast to their father, of course, a figurehead in name only, rarely around or concerned with their lives. Apart from Stephen, who had been working alongside him for far too long.

She eyed Cora in amusement. 'You must have stories to tell about your days as a flight attendant.'

'It was hard work and even lonely at times, because we were always on the move, so our colleagues became our family. I came into the industry after deregulation, which brought lower fares, more flights and less luxury. It's become an everyday means of travel now. But I've spoken to older stewardesses who knew the golden age of flying after the Second World War. Apparently it was a glamorous job. The cabins were much more sophisticated and the girls focused solely on passenger comfort. Back then it was a rare opportunity to see exotic destinations. Smile and stay thin, one of the older trolley dollies told me.'

Amy chuckled. 'Is that what they were called? When life settles down, can I come and do an interview with you?'

'If you think it would be of interest.'

'Absolutely.'

Amy offered to run her mother back to Molly's B&B, but Cora politely refused and phoned for a taxi, leaving as soon as it arrived.

14

Because she hadn't yet heard from Alex, Amy decided on the freedom and exhilaration of her first run in almost a week.

She started warily and slow, rolling and testing her stiff arm and shoulder with each footfall on the soft earth beneath her sneakers. The crisp air nipped at her hands and face, but the sun's feeble late afternoon warmth couldn't pierce the chill. To Amy, the forest was beautiful in any season, even in the dry crackling heat of summer when it provided shade, but especially now on the threshold of winter.

Soft light filtered through the surrounding black ironbark woodland with its dark sombre mood, the cool air filled with the shrill sounds of birds feeding on gum blossom nectar.

Today, her run focused on a mission. In a manner she had yet to determine, somehow Amy wanted to repay Augie Temple for saving her in the tunnel. Without his bush instinct, she might have remained undiscovered for much longer, if at all, and her life threatened or lost. That misfortune didn't bear thought.

She knew the old man had shunned the modern world, only occasionally venturing into the Gully for basic supplies, giving the impression that he not so much preferred his own company but simply the isolation and harmony of nature. This bush reserve in particular.

So what did one gift another such quiet human being with humble needs? Amy was at a loss, so it was with a lighter heart as she approached that she saw him through the trees, hovering in the doorway of his simple bushland hut. Rough-hewn timber with a veranda across one side that faced toward the walking trail where she ran, an open campfire further out circled by stones. She knew from her many previous regular runs, smoke and low orange flames always flickered from within, except in the height of summer. It was illegal and criminal madness in that season to light any naked flame when all around and underfoot was crunchy and parched with heat.

In the past, since she had taken possession of the run-down cabin and moved in to renovate, taking the physical pleasure of a steady jog along the bush tracks winding through the reserve, she might catch a glimpse of Augie in the trees or near his hut. Then she might lift a hand, smile or nod, but pass by.

This morning she waved, stopped to catch her breath and slowly walked toward him, for the first time ever intruding on his modest home. He took the two broad log steps down from the door and she thought she noticed the hint of a smile amid his shaggy moustache and beard.

'Morning,' she called out as she approached, hands on hips catching her breath.

He grinned and nodded, indicating a camp chair by the fire. Notorious for his lack of conversation, Amy plunged ahead, stating yet again the depth of her gratitude for his rescue and her concern as to how she could possibly thank him.

'You're here,' he mumbled. 'That's all I need.'

Amy puzzled over his words, uttered more personally than she would have thought, suggesting a connection between them that had developed since the tunnel.

Glancing about his rustic pioneer surroundings, she grinned. 'To many people these days who prefer living a more comfortable life, it wouldn't seem like it.' Amy hesitated before asking, 'Cora said to ask why you live out here.'

'Did she, now?' He stared into the small fire. 'I have family in the area.'

'Oh!' Who knew? Amy had never entertained more than a passing interest in this edge-of-civilisation dweller, so her attention and journalistic instinct kicked into play. This promised to be fascinating and potentially newsworthy.

'You don't remember me, do you, lass?' he prompted quietly.

Shaking her head, Amy felt confronted and confused. 'I've always known you lived out here on the fringe of town.'

'Ah, you were right small when it happened,' he murmured in reflection as if to himself.

Amy prepared herself for some sad tale of his past that had reduced him to living rough and in seclusion, feeling mercenary for thinking this could lead to a newspaper article and how much she would love an in-depth interview.

'We're descended from the Scottish Randalls

of Orkney from way back in the Middle Ages.'

We? Amy wasn't altogether sure of her heritage. She only knew her father's ancestors were immigrants at the time of the gold rush, poor families seeking to make their fortune.

'You mean we're somehow related?' Not unreasonable to assume. Many families in town today had ancestors who emigrated to seek gold in the region's early days of bush civilisation. Descendants still lived in the area.

He didn't answer her question, just rambled. 'I've never liked the indoors. That's how it started. I've always preferred mucking about outside. Me driving wagons like me father and grandfather before me. When the motors took over, that's when I came unstuck.'

Amy grew intrigued by the old man's reminiscences and couldn't ignore the coincidence. 'Were you somehow connected or employed in our family's transport company?'

'Once.'

'Really?'

He turned slowly toward her, eyes twinkling out from his weathered face. 'I owned it, lass. Handed it over to David.'

All of Amy's senses stalled. 'My father bought it from you? I thought he inherited it from his father?'

'He did.'

Augie turned back to the fire, folded his hands patiently between his knees and waited until the truth sank in.

'But if he's your son, then you're my — grandfather.'

'Aye, lass.'

'And you saved me,' she whispered.

He nodded. 'I sensed somethin' that morning I can't explain. Me heart broke when I found ye.'

'But we don't have the same name?'

'We do. I never use it. I'm August Temple Randall.'

This mysterious old man was family! And then the deeper she dared allow them to flood back, a long-buried and hazy curtain began to rise, allowing images to return. She placed one hand over her trembling mouth, blinked madly at the tears, and hesitantly reached out. With the back of her hand, she fondly stroked the side of his beard. Almost thirty years ago she had been a mere toddler and he, it seemed, one of her first memories.

'Poppy?' she whispered. God. It was so long ago and so vague, she had always imagined the forgotten visions were only dreams.

Augie's hand reached out and covered hers, a sparkle of moisture in his green eyes, too. 'Aye, lass,' he managed to say, equally moved to emotion.

Amy still couldn't get her head around the reality that this precious old man reduced to living like a hermit was her grandfather! 'Being older, I wonder if Stephen remembers, too?'

He shrugged. 'Mebbe.'

'And our parents have known all this time!' Augie nodded. 'Whenever we asked, they just said you left and never came back.'

'I couldn't manage the business, so I handed it over to him. He were ashamed of me, so I kept me distance but stayed close to watch you children grow up.'

'What happened to your wife? Our grand-mother? I don't remember her at all.'

'Well, you wouldn't, lass.' He paused. 'Ah my Rosie Amelia. She — '

'Wait,' Amy interrupted. 'Amelia? That's my name.'

'Cora named you for her. She died young. I weren't much of a father for a long time after my Rosie passed. That's what took the heart out of me life and why David was an only child. I didn't care for the business anymore, didn't mind it like I should've. Soon as David was old enough he rescued it and took it on. I was happy to leave it all to him. Saw a few acres here for sale on the edge of the reserve and bought them. Lived in a tent till I could build me hut. Been home ever since.'

'I can't believe you haven't been included in the family. Now that I think about it . . . ' She frowned. ' . . . years ago, Dad did mention once that our grandmother had an early death and you left. Said he didn't know where you were, which I know as a lie now, of course. Not sure I can forgive him for that.'

'Aye. I drifted for a few years but I found me way back when I heard David married and you kids came along. Gave me a reason to stay.'

Amy shuffled her camp chair closer and sent him a meaningful glance, feeling an unbidden growing fondness for the town hermit she now was proud to know as her dearest family. 'Would you have wanted us kids to know?'

'Mebbe sometimes, but it probably worked out better for everyone this way.'

'Better for who? I would have loved to have you in my life.'

'Well, you were, really. Pounding the tracks here through the bush. I love seeing you run. Watched you grow up and be bush kids here with your brother and that policeman. Nice bloke, that Alex Hammond. Don't come from much but made something of himself.'

'Yes, he has.' That was a whole other story which she would chat to him about some other time. Today felt just for the two of them. Special. 'Your wedding photo is still above the sitting room fireplace. I know you were much younger then, but you don't look anything like your portrait.'

'Mebbe without me beard?' he stroked it.

Amy loved his quiet sense of humour and had a sudden thought. 'Would you be prepared to trim it for a family wedding?'

'Yours?'

Amy nodded. 'Uh huh.'

Augie's eyes twinkled. 'Didn't know you were engaged, lass.'

She leaned closer until they touched shoulders. 'I'm not. Yet. But don't tell Alex.'

Augie shook his head and chuckled. 'Reckoned you was always going to be a mischief.'

'Maybe I've inherited it from my grandfather,' she teased.

'Well your father never laughed much. He was a serious boy.'

'Mum has a hidden humour she kept under

wraps. She's divorcing Dad.'

'Figured. My son is a selfish, driven man, like his own grandfather. My old man pushed me into the business but I didna like it.'

'How old were you when you married?'

'Nearly thirty. Set eyes on me Rosie and knew she was the one.'

Amy reached over and held his hand. 'I'm sorry. Sounds like you cared for her deeply.'

'Only way. All in.'

'So if Dad's almost sixty then you must be — ninety?' she said unbelievingly.

'Nigh on.'

'My God, we must have a celebration. When's your birthday?'

'September.'

Spring. Amy reflected on that for a moment and then a thrill rushed through her from head to toe. 'Leave it with me,' she said, standing up. 'We'll think of something.'

★ ★ ★

After the Melbourne squad had left and headed back to the city, transporting Kelly Randall with them, Alex was just getting back into his police cruiser when he spotted Stephen about to enter the pub.

'Hey, mate. How you doing?'

'One day at a time.'

'I've seen you looking better.'

'The barman introduced me to some nasty stuff last night. Word's spreading and thought they were helping.'

'You going to Melbourne for Kelly's hearing?'

Stephen shook his head. 'Never want to see her again, mate. I don't owe her a thing.'

'Your call. If she pleads guilty, there won't be a trial. Judge will just weigh it all up and pass down her sentence.'

'Don't care, mate. Know it sounds hard, but I think that's what I need to become.'

Alex slapped him on the back. 'You couldn't be tough if you tried.'

'I'm in no mood to argue.'

'Great. While you're so amenable, I'm about to finish my shift and head out to Amy's cabin. Just a heads-up that I intend to marry your sister.'

Stephen shook his head. 'Damn, Hammond, are you sure? She can be a handful.'

'I know it. Wouldn't have her any other way.'

'Well, shit, Hammond, that's the best news of the year and hard to beat.'

'Your approval means everything, mate.'

Stephen shook his head and grinned. 'Brother-in-law now, huh? Thanks for hiding her out and all your support these past few days.'

'No problem.'

'I think she plans on working from home for a few days. Needs quiet time out there in the bush,' Stephen hinted.

'Be my pleasure to keep her company.'

They slapped each other on the back in a quick man hug.

'By the way,' Alex said, turning around again as they parted, 'congratulations on moving back into your chosen profession.'

'Thanks, mate. Had a board meeting with the old man and directors earlier, sorting out the transition of me leaving. Having dinner tonight with my new employer, Bernie, and his wife.'

'All the best. Hear Lucy Slater's a damn fine cook.'

15

Amy finished her afternoon run, uplifted by the incredible revelation that Augie Temple was, in fact, her Randall grandfather.

Back at the cabin, she showered and changed. So much incredible stuff was happening. She still hadn't heard from Alex, which tugged at her heart with impatience, so she curled up on her sofa by the fire and phoned Stephen, relating the amazing news about Augie Temple being their grandfather.

Like her, he, too, recalled vague memories about the old man.

'The folks knew about Poppy but never told us,' Amy grumbled. 'I bet Dad insisted and Mum would have done what he wanted but not perhaps what she felt in her heart.'

'Maybe in a week or two we should try and coax him out of the bush to your cabin for a family get-together.'

'Sure. We could hardly have it out at Windarrah. Poppy would be way out of his comfort zone. Besides, since Dad deliberately kept his father a secret from us, he probably wouldn't approve.'

'I agree. The past week was a challenge we've all been dealt that will only make us stronger.'

'I hope so. Especially for you. How did your meetings go today?'

'Randall Transport is in the process of

changeover. Dad's unhappy, of course. Furious is probably a better word. Then I'm officially joining Bernie's office as soon as possible. When he's ready, I'll buy the practice. I'm inclined to think he'll do that sooner than planned because it will provide him with a nice little nest egg for his retirement. But for now I'll just ease my way into the business. Might need to employ another law clerk. His present woman is overwhelmed with the workload.'

'So glad everything's on track and happening for you. You and Mum and I have had a chat, but I feel the need to go see Father out at Windarrah. Would you be interested in coming along?'

'I've already had words with him in the office today. He knows my position and thoughts on it all.'

Considering Stephen was leaving the company, Amy had a fair idea what they might be. Like her, disappointment and failed leadership as head of their family. His former public and private reputation of the upstanding local citizen now shot to pieces. Their father would have to live with that.

Because David was a busy man, she phoned Randall Transport to arrange a time. Incredibly, he claimed to be leaving the office already, and it was only five. So within ten minutes Amy pulled up in front of the family homestead. Her father's luxurious Range Rover four-wheel drive was already parked in front of the triple garage.

Crunching across the raked gravel, Amy let herself in through the back porch.

'Dad?' She moved through to the drawing

room to find her father standing alone and lost in the cold and dim of his country mansion. Looking utterly defeated. 'Hi.'

Unsmiling, he acknowledged her with a nod, swilling the amber liquid in his brandy balloon.

Amy flicked on the electric log fire, noticed the fully stocked liquor tray, then sauntered into the huge country pantry she had always envied, noting bottles of every description chilled in the wine fridge. She chose a light chardonnay and poured herself a glass before wandering back to join him.

From the strain on his face and hunched shoulders, it was apparent his daughter-in-law's betrayal and Cora's separation had hit her father hard. Amy couldn't feel any pity for him. Being the powerhouse for which he was renowned, it might take a while for David Randall to contemplate his past lapses or even feel any remorse, but she had no doubt he would recover.

Since her father had clammed up without even an *Are you okay?* Amy didn't know where to start, so she jumped right in.

'You sit in the front pew of church most Sundays as though you own it and yet treated Helen Simpson like dirt. I don't understand how you could do that to another human being. Throwing her out? Disowning your responsibility as the father of her child? That's about as unchristian as it gets.' She paused to calm down. 'However we look at it, Kelly's offence was unforgiveable, but she broke because of your cold attitude toward her mother decades ago and, apparently, their shitty life.'

'I'll make it up to you all.'

Amy scoffed in his flushed face. 'Impossible. Helen Simpson is in a nursing home and Kelly is in prison. Nothing will ever compensate. The damage is done. You can't make the truth go away. This time, money won't buy your way out. I could have been killed. How would you have made that up to Mum and Stephen?' *And Alex*, she thought silently to herself. And possible future grandchildren. 'None of us will forget what happened. We all have to live with the consequences. Especially your son,' she said roughly, struggling to control her anger, feeling the deepest empathy for her brother most of all.

No apology or defence would redeem an event triggered by his selfish actions all those years ago nor erase its history and repercussions now embedded in all their lives.

David Randall drained his glass and poured another. Amazingly, he seemed lost for words with little to say. Amy decided while she was on a roll, she would just keep going, get this confrontation over with and leave.

Taking a deep breath, she took another sip of wine and managed to say more calmly, 'I'm only standing here because my grandfather saved me.'

He jolted in surprise at her words and straightened his shoulders. So, he hadn't been told yet. Cora was certainly making a clean break. Once she would have kept him up to date with family happenings because he was never around when they occurred. Not anymore. She wondered if that would cause even more distance between them in the future, or would he change and make some effort?'

'I was going to tell you.'

'Only because Mum insisted. That old man is living rough in the bush. At ninety!'

'By choice,' he growled.

'With all your money, you never thought to go visit and see if you could bring him back into our lives? Make him more comfortable in his old age?'

'He preferred to be by himself. He's a loner.'

'Well he seemed quite receptive to company when I went to visit. You could at least have tried. From now on, whether you like it or not, he'll be looked after better and in our lives.'

'He was never a father to me.'

Amy's thoughts exploded into a light-bulb moment. 'Is that what you believe all fathers do? You didn't feel the loss of a father so badly in your own life that you determined to make sure you were there for your own kids?'

His gaze narrowed and grew fierce, his voice rough as he spoke. 'I was eighteen when he left me with a small trucking company on the verge of bankruptcy and walked away.'

'From grief over the early loss of my grandmother.'

'He never liked people. While he hid away in the bush, I built his pathetic failing business into a transport empire with determination and hard work. I didn't have time to be a father!'

'You didn't want to be one.'

Feeling as cool as the wine she had just finished, Amy put her glass back in the kitchen on the way out. But she paused in the wide hallway that led in every direction through the homestead, drawn to the huge portrait that had always sat there. Unassuming. Almost neglected.

In childhood she had asked about the man but was always just casually told he was her Randall grandfather who had left town. Mostly a lie but partly true, since he had anonymously returned. All those wasted years.

Amy stood before his black and white photograph, tears pooling in her eyes, recognising a likeness in the young man now she knew the old one and whispered, 'I'm so sorry, Poppy. I wish I'd pushed and asked more questions about you. But I'm so happy you're alive and we can all begin to get to know you.'

Overcome with emotion, Amy barely heard her mobile beep as she walked out into the cold evening air, the twilight of her arrival having been overtaken by darkness.

In the car, she glanced at her phone. Her heart raced. Alex. Perfect timing. He was free.

★　★　★

Amy had not long returned home from Windarrah when she saw a flash of headlights in the driveway announcing Alex's arrival.

Finally alone, their individual news could wait until tomorrow. She had plans for tonight and they didn't include too much talking. Memorable and intimate came to mind. Man, was she hanging out for the intimate bit. She'd seen some of the physical half-dressed Alex Hammond this past week and wanted to see the rest.

208

All of it. Thinking of him completely naked, she fanned herself against the rush of heat that flooded through her body.

When her walking dreamboat strolled in wearing tight jeans and a sweater pushed up to the elbows, she didn't have time to move across the room to greet him.

He threw his car keys on the kitchen bench, kicked off his boots and prowled toward her, looking wonderfully dangerous.

His smile stopped her heart. Crushed tight against his athletic body and kissed to distraction was a great start. Neither of them mentioned or had any thought for food. Except the kind that fed the heart and soul. Amy was beginning to understand it as love.

From the guarded rebellious boy she first knew, Alex Hammond had grown, left town and returned. No longer the brooding high school graduate. A changed mature man in looks and attitude, lean and fit, possessed of an easy confidence that created an aura of controlled stillness around him.

Amy roughly pushed her hands up into his hair, blown away by the miracle of a girl's dream coming true. That the Fossicker's Gully cop, her forever fantasy wish and childhood crush, returned her adult passion in equal measure.

The big hands stroking a trail over her curves, inflamed her already pulsing senses, teasing and awakening every inch, heating her skin, rocking her body to its core.

'I think we need to get a room,' he growled with heavy-eyed intent.

'You know where it is.'

Amy squealed with laughter as, with the smallest amount of effort, he scooped her up into his arms. Impressive. She was no pixie.

With her hands looped around his neck and nibbling the dip of his neck as he climbed the stairs, Amy forgot all the recent horrors and secrecy to focus on this moment in her life that she would always remember.

With restrained patience, they undressed each other in the half-light of romantic shadows. Moonlight filtered into the bedroom, gleaming on Alex's toned and sculpted torso. He couldn't hide the deep desire in his burning gaze as Amy felt his warm hands slowly caressing her shoulders and arms, finally seeking her full breasts, their hard buds hungry with longing.

Her eager hands brushed a trail over his muscled chest. With their naked bodies pressed together, their lips met in thirsty kisses, fuelling their need. The night around them was lost and their hot sensual world exploded.

Alex cupped her behind. Amy groaned and wrapped her legs around him. He carried her to the bed and with gentleness and reverence began a slow and powerful loving that left her breathless. They dozed, spooned together and made love again.

Eventually, Amy fell into a deep sleep. So it shocked her in the middle of the night when she found herself awake and restless. Anxious, even. Trying not to disturb the gorgeous shadowy image of the man beside her, she slid out of bed and shrugged on her robe.

Under the heady influence of Alex Hammond, Amy had finally allowed her body to relax after the week's ordeals and challenges. Which meant the guard she had been holding up to the world came crashing down and her emotions surfaced. Staring out of the upstairs window to the dark and shadowy surrounding bushland, she stood quietly weeping.

She should have been happy in the wake of Alex's expert lovemaking. The man sure knew his stuff and he was all hers. She had willingly given him everything of herself. Body and soul, she was his. So why this sadness?

'Amy?' Alex said softly into the dim room.

Trembling and miserable, she half turned, feeling so loved yet broken.

He was out of bed and, standing behind, wrapped her in his arms. 'I've been watching you all week,' he murmured. 'After Kelly kidnapped you last weekend and the sting this morning, you're in emotional shock.'

Amy laid her head back against him, his warm stubbled cheek brushing hers, listening to his deep calming voice.

'Give yourself time for your body and mind to work through it all. To come to a slow realisation of what has happened to you.'

'Don't leave me,' she pleaded.

'Never.'

'I've just had a horrible dream.'

'You'll get flashbacks. Now you know what to expect, you'll be ready if it happens again.'

'Will it?'

'Possibly.'

She turned into his big safe arms, just needing to be held.

'I make a mean hot chocolate,' he murmured against her hair, drawing away. Amy felt deprived of the comfort and heat of his body. 'Don't go anywhere.' He kissed her on the nose.

With that backside in tight jeans, bare chest and feet, Amy wanted to pull him back into bed. 'While you're here, I'm not going anywhere.'

'After tonight,' he chuckled, 'I'm never leaving.'

Amy went back to bed and snuggled down under the covers, feeling cheered. When Alex returned with two steaming mugs of their creamy soothing drinks, they huddled together and pulled the doona up around them.

'Mind if I talk about Kelly?' he asked softly.

Amy shook her head. It was if Alex read her mind, because she now felt a need to talk about that very issue.

'If she pleads guilty,' he began, 'she will be considered convicted. In about six weeks, a brief is presented with statements and records of interviews before the committal hearing. The court appoints a hearing date and the judge will decide a penalty. He may need time to consider it, so Kelly will remain in custody. In the meantime, I should think she will be taken for a psychiatric assessment and possible treatment.

'The maximum penalty for her crime is 25 years.' Amy gasped. 'But the standard sentence is mostly about 11. Eight years non-parole, so she would probably only serve that amount of time.'

'And lose a decade of her life,' Amy

murmured. 'Where did you go this morning before the sting was about to start?'

'Jim was home from prison.'

'How did that go?'

'Bit tense. Nothing I haven't handled before.' He grinned. 'Selma laid down some rules and put him on notice. Lisa and little Gracie have moved in with her. Not sure what that means for her relationship with Mick. I guess Lisa may be looking for work now. I didn't ask. Kept thinking of you waiting alone in the tunnel for the sting and just wanted to get back to you.'

'I hope it all works out for them. Actually . . . ' Amy frowned, blew on her hot drink and took another sip. 'Stephen will be looking for help when he starts with Bernie. Does Lisa have any office experience?'

'Not sure. I think she was in hospitality. I'll ask.'

'At least she'll know how to make them a decent coffee. I'm sure Bernie's secretary, Maisie, will give her some training. Might be worth checking out. She has nothing to lose.'

'Been thinking to have a word with Harry down at the garage about getting Billy started in a trade. He hates books but he's damn good with his hands. That boy can fix anything.' He glanced down at her. 'How did your family all pull up after this week?'

Amy groaned. 'Except for Mum, they're all a bit of a broken mess. At least Dad is. Stephen seems determined to forget he was ever married.' She paused. 'Kelly must have been desperate to plot such extreme revenge.'

'Hell, no family's perfect. Look at mine. I've learned the hard way that I can't save everyone. Jim and Buddy are serial offenders. They don't want to change. So I just stand up for those more vulnerable that need my support and do the best I can with the others.

'In a certain way,' he went on, 'being a policeman is like being part of a family, too. You can't change the world but you still get to help people. There's stress and demands in a large police station; drugs often end up in violence. We pull people out of smashed cars, injured or dead. It can exhaust your soul. But those times where we make small differences to people's lives are rewarding.

'The city's like another country. You're just another body in the crush. In a small-town community like here in Fossicker's Gully, we know people. Personal connection to a place means a lot.'

'Yeah. Know what you mean,' Amy murmured, captivated by Alex's voice. 'I feel it too. I can't explain why, but I've always been drawn back here somehow. There'll be gossip around town for a while but I'm sure we'll weather it.' She yawned, set aside her finished mug and sighed. 'Besides, my new boyfriend is a cop. He'll watch out for me.'

'Hope I'm more than that,' he drawled.

'Well I have been otherwise occupied this past week, but I'm sure we can come to some arrangement. How much more do you want?' She held her breath.

'Won't lie to you, Amy. In the past I've always

214

done casual, but with you I want commitment. Everything. For life.'

'That's a serious long-term wish list.'

'I'm aware it's a big ask, but do you think I'll achieve it?'

'Oh trust me, Alexander Hammond, you're a slow burn yourself, and it took a while, but your prospects are looking mighty good.'

'I'm onto it now.'

'None too soon.'

'Don't give me lip or I might have to enforce some laws.'

'Like the sound of that. I'll break any law you want to make that happen.'

Alex chuckled, deep and throaty. His empty mug clattered to the floor as he grabbed a squirming Amy who had snaked her legs around his and nestled against his body. He kissed her long and slow and gentle, her anxiety spent, this man her whole safe and secure world now.

It still felt early when the first soft shafts of morning light woke her to see Alex propped on an elbow, gazing on her with pure adoration in his eyes.

She smiled.

'I love you,' he whispered.

'Back at you, Hammond,' she said dreamily, rubbing her eyes. 'I know you don't have much time. You're on duty soon.' She sat up, shaking with excitement, and blurted out about Augie being her grandfather.

'What!' Alex laughed, lacing his hands behind his head. 'That's unbelievable.'

Amy was distracted by all that bare chest but

felt secure in what she was about to ask. 'Long story short, Poppy exiled himself from the family, so I have something I need to discuss with you.'

Ever since being hidden with Alex in his flat, stunned by their amazing almost instant chemistry and his absolute, if originally sceptical, support, she had marvelled at the swift progress of a relationship that had blown into something magical in only a week.

Of course, for her it had been humming inside for years. The idolatry, sense of forbidden awe at the sight of such a dreamboat of a local town bad boy being mates with her older brother. Being her usual stubborn self and doggedly tagging along wherever the two boys explored on weekends and school holidays just so she could be around him. So the explosion of romance so speedily springing into life was not so sudden at all. And perhaps, as she had so quietly learned from Alex, not such a surprise for him either.

'I know you haven't asked me yet, but how long before we marry?'

His already reverent attention sharpened. 'Amelia May Randall, where is this heading?'

'Just keep being agreeable, okay?' She clenched her hands together and pressed closer against him. Every. Adorable. Inch. Skin against skin. 'You love me, right?'

'So I've said.'

'And you hinted a long-term thing. Like becoming permanent partners? Down the track,' she added hastily.

'Yep, believe I did.'

216

'Or sooner?' she probed.

'Whatever we decide, I guess.' Alex slid higher against his pillow and crossed his arms over his impressive bare chest, agreeably amused. 'To be honest, I haven't considered it yet.'

Amy knew a moment of panic. She'd thought this all out last night. Was she moving too fast? Had she read him wrong? 'You haven't?'

'I'm beginning to understand it's probably closer than I think,' he drawled.

'Yeah, we're kinda running out of time.'

'You can't be pregnant.'

'No,' she chuckled, 'but we'll have fun trying when the time comes. So, say, three months?' She wrinkled her nose, a whisper of pleading hope in her voice.

'Whatever *you* decide?' he suggested.

'Great!' Amy beamed. 'So, September then?'

'The date's clearly special for some reason, right?'

'Very. It's Poppy's ninetieth birthday and I can't think of a better day to marry.'

'I could remind you that you haven't been asked.'

'Oh come on, Hammond. This is the twenty-first century. Times are changing. Keep up.'

Epilogue

Running through the nature reserve along familiar tracks, Amy's sneakers pounded on the soft warm earth of spring. Beneath the canopy of ironbark forest, the bush understorey was coming to life. The first golden wattles were appearing and the swift parrots gradually migrating, deserting their winter home.

The first early rays of sunshine crested the horizon, revealing a veil of gossamer fog draping itself in the canopy above. The sun's warmth would soon dissolve the mist, but a plume of steam still trailed into the air each time she exhaled a breath.

Fossicker's Gully was slowly recovering after its recent sensational crime rocked the community to its foundations, no doubt a topic of conversation in the town's history for years to come.

'Hey, Poppy.' She waved and smiled as she jogged past his hut. 'Back in fifteen. Have that kettle boiling.'

With a little arm-twisting, her grandfather had actually agreed to a few more comfortable improvements to his rustic dwelling, but still jealously guarded his isolation. And his family were now able to watch out for him. He looked better, Amy believed, because whether the stubborn gentle gold fossicker admitted it or not, he was happier.

Either Stephen or Amy picked him up and drove him to the monthly dinner at Cora's simple miner's cottage in town, where everyone brought food and gathered for a catch-up feast. Her mother glowed with an inner peace that filled Amy's heart to see.

David Randall ploughed on with business as usual as if nothing had happened, his oblivion astounding, and only occasionally joined the family dinner, often citing pressure of work for non-attendance.

Jim Hammond had mostly given up crime but was seen leaning on the hotel bar every day instead. Buddy Hammond managed to keep his nose clean, at least as far as his oldest brother knew, but Alex had his doubts. Billy Hammond grumbled as he studied for his high school exams but was actually looking forward to starting an apprenticeship with Harry at the garage.

Lisa Hammond was employed at Slater and Randall law offices under the close tuition and guidance of Maisie Gray.

Gwennie stunned the townsfolk by retiring, so Julie Hammond now owned the salon, snipping a short back and sides for her senior male clients as they read the *Gully Standard*, treating the more mature ladies of the district to their weekly shampoo and set, or the young girls the latest colours and styles.

Amy could hardly believe the wedding and ninetieth birthday celebration were next week.

Because Amy and Alex had invited half the people of Fossicker's Gully, their casual ceremony and buffet banquet with a very special birthday party afterwards were all being held in Windarrah gardens.

Amy's dress hung in the closet of her old bedroom in the homestead, safely hidden away from the groom's prying eyes, because he now lived with Amy. Whatever Alex wore on the day would be heart-stopping but irrelevant, because whenever she saw or thought of him, the town cop simply took her breath away.

She couldn't wait to formally announce her commitment to sharing her life with the man she loved with all her heart. Then enjoy the celebration for a special and beloved grandfather who had re-emerged in all their lives.

For Amy, the future held nothing but promise and love, with the prospect of children who would be closely watched and cherished, especially by their great-grandfather.

Other titles published by Ulverscroft:

EVERY YESTERDAY

Noelene Jenkinson

New South Wales, Australia: Three sisters reconnect and forge new lives. Coming home to attend her mother's funeral, Daisy Sheldon discovers fond memories at the childhood cottage she must now sell, and decides to settle in the nearby town of Inlet Creek. But can a passionate romance with an older man offer the future she wants? After a tragedy, Maddie is torn: should she stay and help her father run the family's sheep farm, or pursue a new relationship with a man of mystery? When he learns about her past, will she face rejection? And the death of a dear relative is the catalyst that gives Lilly the time and space to rethink her life — and the need for a fresh start, leaving England for Inlet Creek and the comforts of family and home.